Secret Summer Dreams

Other books by Beverly Lewis

Holly's First Love
Sealed with a Kiss
The Trouble with Weddings

Secret Summer Dreams

BEVERLY ♥ LEWIS

ZondervanPublishingHouse
Grand Rapids, Michigan

A Division of HarperCollins*Publishers*

Requests for information should be addressed to:
Zondervan Publishing House
Grand Rapids, Michigan 49530

Lewis, Beverly, 1949–
Secret summer dreams / BeveryLews.
p. cm.
Summary: Despite her mother's objectsions, thirteen-year-old Holly wants to visit her long-unseen father in California, not only to renew their relationship, but to talk to him about the Lord.
ISBN 0-310-38061-8
[1. Mothers and daughters—Fiction. 2. Christian life—-Fiction.]
I. Title.
PZ7.L58464Se 1993
[Fic]—dc20
93-18053
CIP
AC

Printed in the United States of America

95 96 97 / LP / 10 9 8 7 6 5

To Jane B. Jones,
my dear mother and friend,
who blesses me with an understanding heart
And
To her namesake, my Janie . . .
dreamer of heart-dreams,
secret and not-so-secret

♥ Author's Note ♥

Hugs to my cool consultants—Shanna, Amy, Julie, Janie, Becky, Allison, and Niki.

Cheers to my Monday night SCBWI group, including Mary Erickson, Vicki Fox, Carol Reinsma, and Peggy Marshall, who offered valuable assistance on the manuscript, as did Barbara Birch, Madalene Harris, Lorraine Pintus, Barb Reinhard, and my husband, Dave.

Big thank-you's to my editors Lori Walburg and Dave Lambert for their ongoing encouragement and enthusiasm.

Special thanks to my friend Carolene Robinson for her expert medical information.

"Holly Meredith!"

I woke with a start. It was Andie Martinez, my best friend. She stood in the aisle of the bus, brown eyes wide, staring down at me. Jared Wilkins and three guys from the choir tour leaned over the seats of our chartered bus to get in on the action. They laughed as Andie, speechless, pointed at my hair.

Then I felt it. A tickling sensation, as if a giant spider were crawling step by hideous step through my hair. I froze. "Andie, what is it?" I asked through clenched teeth.

"I–I'm not sure," she said, her eyes fixed on my ponytail.

The creepy crawling continued. "Get it off me, Andie!"

"Hand me a Kleenex," Jared said.

"Not you, Jared!" I squealed. "Don't *you* touch me."

"Where's a scissors?" one of the boys joked. "Maybe we could get the thing to crawl down her hair, and cut it out."

"No, Andie!" I shrieked. "Not that!" I wasn't sure which was worse, losing my long hair or enduring this thing nesting in it.

"What's going on back there?" the choir director called.

Jared shouted, "Holly has something in her hair and she's freaking out."

By now the thing-a-ma-bug had moved to the top of my head.

"Look, she's turning white," Andie said. "Someone help!"

"Quick, grab my camera," Jared yelled as I sat there, trembling.

A flash of light blinded me. Seconds later a box of tissues came flying. Jared caught it and tossed several to Andie. "Here, if you stuff enough of these in your hand, you'll never even touch it," he said.

Just then Danny Myers walked down the bus aisle. Unlike most boys in junior high, his head nearly touched the ceiling of the bus. "What's Holly—?"

He stopped in mid-sentence when he saw *it*—the whatever-it-was—having a holiday in my hair. Before I could move, he reached over, and with a quick flick of his finger, a velvety green beetle flew off my head and towards an open window.

"It's just a June bug," he said. "Are you okay, Holly?"

"A–a *what* bug?" I said, beginning to relax, feeling comfortable as usual around Danny. I pulled my ponytail around and ran my fingers through it.

"Looks like you need a handful of snickerdoodles," Danny said, laughing.

"My all-time favorite cookies," I said, surprised. He was a walking memory chip! "How did you remember?"

His green eyes turned serious. "I make it a point to recall crucial information—such as the names of important junk foods." He smirked, then we broke into laughter.

I shivered, still feeling that creepy-crawly June bug on my head. Danny must have noticed my concern. "Don't worry, Holly, it's gone." He ran a hand through his own auburn hair. "Next time, scream or something. Don't hold it in or you could pass out."

Passing out, otherwise known as fainting, was not an option. Not *this* time. During the seventh grade musical, last winter, I'd fainted off the next-to-top riser. Thanks to Andie, I survived the whole embarrassing scene.

Now, she sat down across the aisle from me. "I'm real sorry I freaked over that bug, Holly. I wasn't much help, was I?"

"Forget it." I rubbed my head to get rid of the tickly feeling.

"You were so together," Andie said. "Me? I would've behaved like a mad woman. Shouting, hysteria, you name it."

I giggled. "I can just imagine."

"Can you believe it? Jared took your picture with that nasty bug in your hair." Andie squeezed her chubby legs past mine and sat down at the window seat next to me.

"Let's not talk about him." Our former heartthrob, Jared Wilkins, had almost destroyed our ten-year friendship. Before he moved to Dressel Hills, Colorado, things had always been perfectly cool between Andie and me. But soon we weren't speaking to each other. Worse—our friendship ripped apart. And fast—the way Grandma's seam ripper zaps threads. Before we knew it, Andie and I were helplessly caught in a vicious love triangle.

Jared was a charmer all right. Brown hair cut in the latest style. Blue eyes with lashes long enough to curl. But looks and charm were *all* he had. Now we knew he was nothing but a two-timing, heartbreaking flirt. Thankfully, Andie and I came to our senses in time to save our friendship.

That was last month. Now things were fabulous between us. They should be. We'd just spent a day at Disneyland, and now we were racing through the dusty Arizona desert on our way to the Grand Canyon!

Andie cleared her throat. "Daydreaming again?"

"Sort of," I said.

She leaned over, whispering in my ear. "You know what I think?"

I grinned back at her. "What?"

"I think Danny Myers likes you."

"Shh, he'll hear you," I whispered, glancing up towards the front of the bus.

"Well?" she said.

"Well, what?"

Andie curled a strand of dark hair around her finger. "I bet you two get together for the skating party next week."

I rolled my eyes. "Where do you come up with this stuff?"

"Just wait and see," she said. "I've caught him watching you, Holly. Ever since we sang at the L.A. chapel."

I stared out the window. Danny Myers wasn't like the other boys in eighth grade. At fourteen and a half, he was much more grown up. More sensitive, too. He'd helped me out when Andie and I weren't getting along. He probably only thought of me as a little sister. That's all.

Andie poked me. "Holly, you're avoiding my question."

I twisted the ends of my hair. "I *forgot* the question."

"Nice try." She inched closer. "Hmm, I think I see Danny Myers in your eyes," she teased.

"Get outta my face." I playfully pushed her away.

She giggled, pulling a brochure from her jeans pocket.

"What's that?"

"Info on the Grand Canyon," she said, smoothing the folds. "I picked it up at our last rest stop."

Jared came down the aisle, stopping at our seats. "Hi again, girls." He laid his hand on the back of my seat and smiled. Andie and I exchanged a quick look.

"Now what?" Andie asked.

"It's lonely in the front of the bus," he said.

Andie stood. Cupping her hands around her eyes, she scanned the front of the bus. Then, with a huge sigh, she sat down. "Looks okay to me. Plenty of boys up there."

I muttered under my breath, "Just no *girls*."

Jared ignored my comment and pointed at Andie's brochure. "Is that what I think it is?"

"Could be," Andie said. "Depends on what you think it is."

"Hmm. Looks like a great place to hike," he said, then headed toward the restroom in the back of the bus.

Andie peered at the information on her brochure. "It says the gorge is 200 miles long. Wow! Who can see that far?"

"Daddy says he goes there when he feels like life is caving in on him," I said softly.

Andie turned to face me. "You must've had a good talk with your dad after our concert the other night," she said, prying in a roundabout way.

"It was weird seeing him again, you know. He's missed the last four years of my life. Says he wants to catch up."

Andie's dark eyebrows shot up. "How *can* he, when he lives in California with his new wife, and you and your mom and Carrie live in Colorado?"

I took a deep breath. "This summer."

Andie gasped. "You're going to California this summer?"

I nodded.

"Your mother will never let you," Andie said. "And neither will I."

"*You* won't?"

"Have you forgotten that we always go camping together? Every summer since second grade! You don't want to go and mess things up, do you?" she demanded.

"I have to do this," I said. "For me."

Andie folded her arms in a huff.

I stared Andie down. "Don't do this," I said. "It'll be hard enough getting Mom to let me go, without you putting me on a guilt trip about it."

"Boring, boring." She put on her best pout. "It'll be boring for you out there. You'll see."

"Andie, listen," I said softly. "Your father lives with you and your family. Mine left when I was in third grade. You'd be curious, too."

"So it's curiosity then?"

"That and other stuff," I said, reluctant to share more.

"Oh, Holly, don't be stubborn. Can't you tell me?"

"Not now," I said, noticing Jared Wilkins coming back from the bus restroom. No way was he going to overhear this conversation.

She ignored me, continuing her guilt campaign. "It'll be the lousiest summer of my life!"

"Shh!" Privacy was impossible on a bus, especially now that Jared had plopped himself down behind us, eavesdropping. I gave Andie a don't-you-dare-say-anything look. She smoothed out her brochure of Grand Canyon National Park while I flipped through the pages of my devotional book.

"What's the verse for today?" Jared asked, peeking around my seat.

I had already tried the polite approach, so I ignored him and kept reading. Why didn't he just evaporate?

"Come on, Holly-Heart, give a guy a chance," he crooned. "We can still be friends. Can't we?"

Without looking up, I said, "Holly-Heart is the nickname my mother gave me. Reserved for relatives and close friends only. Remember?"

Andie glanced over and stifled a giggle.

"Hmm," Jared said. "I don't want to be your relative. But a close friend? That'll work."

I slammed my book shut and whirled around. "I'll be honest with you, Jared. I liked you once. But that's over because I don't trust you. Besides, you made big trouble for Andie and me."

Andie cheered. She forgot it was quiet time for all choir members. When some kids turned around and shushed her, she got as red as the illustrated cliffs on her brochure.

Jared slunk back to his seat like a wounded puppy. Some act.

"Will he ever give up?" I whispered to Andie.

"Persistence is his game," she said. "Now you're a big challenge to him. Maybe if you act a teeny bit interested, he'll leave you alone."

"I can't do that," I said. "It would be a lie."

Andie refolded the brochure. "Let's talk summer, Holly."

I sighed and looked away. *She* was persistent, too.

"Please, Holly, think about it. You're throwing our whole summer away," she whined.

Andie sounded selfish. She was acting like she hadn't heard a thing I'd said before.

"C'mon, let's talk," she pleaded.

"About something else, maybe?" I leaned against the head rest and closed my eyes.

"No fair sleeping. Summer's coming faster than you think."

"Okay," I said, giving in. "Besides the family camping trip, what else do you want to do?"

"A raft trip," she said, sitting on the edge of her seat. "A wild and crazy whitewater raft trip down the Arkansas River. I hear it's outrageous. Imagine the breathtaking thrill of Zoom Flume, Screaming Right, and get this . . . The Widow Maker!"

"Which means girls have to be pretty tough if the guys don't survive," I concluded.

"And," she said her voice growing louder and more excited, "the minimum age is twelve, so you know it's gotta be wild."

Annoyed looks were cast our way by choir members observing Mr. Keller's quiet time. I put my finger to my lips.

Andie slumped down in her seat, curling her chubby legs under her. She grinned. Andrea Martinez—Miss Magnificent Manipulator—had me, and she knew it. Rafting was the one thing I'd been dying to do. An all-day trip down the mighty Arkansas . . . and two weeks of camping with Andie and her family! Irresistible.

Mom's idea of camping was the Holiday Inn without maid service, of course. No chance *she'd* go. But Andie's family? That was a different story. Her twin baby brothers, Donnie and Jon, would stay with their grandma, then off we'd go. Before the arrival of the "double blessing"—as Andie's mom called them—the Martinez family went camping every summer. Thanks to Andie, I got to tag along.

What great summers they were! We always camped high in the Colorado Rockies near the Twin Lakes, nestled like giant mirrors beneath the soaring mountains. There the air smelled of pine trees, and the lakes were so blue it seemed a piece of sky had fallen to the earth. Wispy clouds scurried past snowy mountain peaks, and the summer sun warmed the valleys. It was enough to birth the poet in me.

Andie's father, dashing and comical, kept us in stitches at all times. Summer and laughter seemed to hold hands—at least on camping trips with Andie and her family. Would spending the summer with Daddy be worth all the sacrifices I'd have to make?

The sacrificial list was growing. I'd miss out on

camping with Andie, youth meetings, whitewater rafting, and . . . maybe getting to know Danny Myers! But I wasn't going to let any of it come between me and my secret summer dream—to visit my dad and get to know him, for the first time in four years.

"Quiet time's over! Up and at 'em!" Walking down the aisle of the bus, Mr. Keller clapped his hands to wake up sleeping kids. "We're almost to the Grand Canyon!"

The Grand Canyon! The magical words awakened all thirty of us. Soon the bus was buzzing with excited voices.

I grabbed Andie's Grand Canyon leaflet, tracing the path of the Colorado River. From what I'd read, its treacherous rapids and gigantic boulders made navigation barely possible.

"That's *one* raft trip we can forget about," Andie said as my finger slid along the path the swift river cut through the canyon.

"Guess you'd have to work up to a trip like that," I said.

Andie looked pleased. "So, you *are* thinking about staying home this summer?"

I flashed her a knowing smile. She was sneaky, all right!

Mr. Keller announced that we were welcome to explore the area as long as we didn't go wandering off alone. "Please take someone with you," he said. "I want to return all of you to your families in one piece."

"How dangerous *is* this place?" I asked Andie.

"Can't be too dangerous," she said. "Look at all the people." We peered out the window as the bus inched into an open spot. The parking lot *was* crowded.

"We'll see soon enough," I said, wondering if the Grand Canyon would be any big deal.

We bounded off the bus and headed straight for the lookout area, which was rimmed with a rock wall.

"Fabulous," I said. That's all I could say for the next five minutes, as Andie and I and the rest of the choir stood drinking in the sight.

It was late afternoon, and a golden haze lay over the canyon. Gazing across, I saw the rosy-reds and grey-blues of the cliff-like formations. Dark ravines, gouged out by the river's tortuous path, made me feel small, like a speck in the universe. I felt lost in the canyon's never-endingness. Squinting, I wondered where it ended. Andie was right. Who can see for 200 miles?

I felt Andie's hand on my arm.

"Holly? You okay?" she asked.

I felt frozen. "It's, it's like *forever.*"

"You're right," Danny said. I hadn't noticed him standing right next to me, but Andie had. She threw me a look that said "I told you so."

I ignored her and turned to Danny. "Makes me wonder how God keeps track of everything on this earth," I said. "He even knows how many hairs are on our heads!"

"And when June bugs are gonna dance in them," Andie said, tugging playfully at my ponytail. Then she consulted her brochure. "It says here that the park is almost two thousand square miles, and that there are 290 species of birds that fly between these canyon walls."

Danny pulled out his binoculars and scanned the rocks below. "The smallest animals live in those crevices a mile down," he said. "No way can God be nearsighted!"

Andie and I laughed. Out of the corner of my eye I spotted Jared, standing a few feet away and looking annoyed. Probably jealous of the attention we were giving Danny. *Too bad,* I thought. *He had his chance, and he blew it.*

Danny touched my arm. He was still looking through his binoculars, but he directed my gaze to a ledge far below. "If you look carefully, you'll see a red-tailed hawk," he said, handing the binoculars over to me. He helped me adjust the focus and pointed me in the right direction. "They live in all parts of the canyon, except near damp areas or open water."

Then I spotted it—a fierce, proud bird, perched

on the edge of a cliff. Spreading its wings, it flew away, and I followed it with the binoculars until it disappeared from view.

"That was cool—thanks!" I said, handing the binoculars back to Danny. He smiled and took them from me, then moved closer to the stone wall to peer down the edge of the ravine.

"How does he know all that stuff?" Andie whispered.

"He reads constantly," I said.

"Anyone can read about stuff. How does he remember all of it?" Andie asked.

"Photographic memory, I guess." Admiration filled me as I watched Danny. He had his binoculars up again, slowly scanning the canyon.

The group started to break up. A bunch of kids went to the gift shop to buy souvenirs and candy. Others hung around the coin-operated telescopes. Jared came over and suggested that we hike down into the canyon a short way. "It's safe enough," he said. "And we've got a whole hour. Mr. Keller said we needed to be back on the bus ready to go at six."

"Uh, I don't know about this," I said, looking down at the great abyss.

"C'mon, Holly. Don't be such a scaredy," Andie said. "Where's the trail?" she asked Jared.

"This way." They walked off together, leaving me with Danny.

"Is it safe?" I asked him.

"We won't hike too far," he said, moving up beside me. We followed Jared as he made his way toward the hiking path. "Want to wear these?" Danny asked, pulling the binoculars over his head.

"Sure!"

He handed them to me and our fingers touched when I took them. A strange, giddy feeling shot like an arrow straight to my heart. Was I falling for Danny Myers? *Don't think such a thing,* I told myself.

We hurried to the trailhead where Jared and Andie waited. I peered hesitantly down the path. The blacktopped path zigzagged down the side of the cliff, and it wasn't exactly level. In fact, it looked like a forty-degree angle to me!

"Stay close to this," Andie said, patting the reddish rock wall on the left.

I headed down, one hand touching the wall, my tennies skidding a little on the steep path. Keeping my eyes on the trail, I tried not to think about the sheer dropoff to the right of me. Jared led the way, followed by Andie, then me, and last, Danny. I was glad he was behind me. Somehow it made me feel safer.

After completing several switchbacks, we stopped to gaze at the beauty around us. I made sure my back was safely up against the canyon wall before I pulled out the binoculars and scanned the slopes just below the canyon rim.

There was a slight movement. I adjusted the focus. A deer—with antlers and the largest ears I'd ever seen! I caught my breath.

"What is it, Holly?" Danny asked.

"I think it's a deer . . . but it's got huge ears," I

said, watching as the deer moved gracefully along the cliff, grazing.

Danny said, "It must be a mule deer."

"Hee, haw!" Jared brayed like a donkey. "Let's see!" He pushed between Danny and me.

"Wait your turn, Jared," I said, still gazing through the lenses. The deer had lifted his head and seemed to be staring at me, his head cocked, his eyes alert. I inched forward, intent on the deer.

"Hurry up," Jared said in a silly voice, pulling on the strap to the binoculars.

"Just a minute!" I snarled, swinging away from him. As I did, I lost my balance. The binoculars fell from my hands and my feet slipped away from me. Desperate, I grabbed for the canyon wall—anything—

Andie screamed. "Holly! No!"

For a terrifying second the sky spun above me.

Then a strong hand grabbed my arm. "I've got you, Holly!" Danny's other hand took my arm and pulled me away from the dropoff. "Here." He set me against the canyon wall. Shaking, I leaned against the rock, my hands wet with fear. I refused to look down into the great chasm below.

Andie took my hand. "Holly!" she said. "Are you all right?"

I nodded slowly, trying to catch my breath. She and Danny looked at me, concern written on their faces. Jared hung back—knowing it was his fault, I suppose.

Closing my eyes, I took a few more breaths. I could still feel my feet slipping out from beneath me—the sky tilting to meet me . . . I shivered and opened my eyes. "I'm fine, really!" I said when Andie and Danny didn't look convinced. "Danny saved my life."

I pressed my hands against the canyon wall. The solid rock felt reassuring under my fingertips. Suddenly, I remembered. "The binoculars! They're gone!"

Jared held them high over his head. "Never fear, Jared's here!"

"That's what I'm afraid of," Danny said, frowning. "If you hadn't been here, clowning around like that, nothing would have happened."

"Well, let's hear it for Mr. Responsible! If Holly hadn't been looking through *your* binoculars, this wouldn't have happened either."

It was a stupid comparison, but Danny didn't say anything. They just glared at each other.

"Can we go back now?" I asked, still a little shook up.

Jared started to argue, but Danny gave him a stern look and he stopped.

"I'll go behind you, Holly, and catch you if you slip," Danny said.

"Good," I said. Jared led the way again, with Andie following. My knees still shook from the close call as I started up the trail, watching my step and staying close to the right side of the path, near the wall. Whenever I even glimpsed the edge of the trail, I shivered deep inside.

The climb up took longer than going down. Soon I was breathing hard.

"Can you make it all right?" Danny asked from behind me.

"Yeah," I said, not turning my head. We didn't talk the rest of the way. I was still too rattled to concentrate on anything except getting out of there.

At last we arrived at the top. I turned around for one last look, then the four of us headed for the bus.

A tassel-eared squirrel darted across our path. We stopped to watch as it shimmied over the rocks and disappeared. "What kind of squirrel is that?" I asked. "I've never seen anything like it in Colorado."

"I have an animal guide back in the bus," Danny said. "We can look it up there, if you want."

"Sure," I said. Andie flashed me a knowing smile. I knew what she was thinking.

Mr. Keller was standing beside the bus door counting the kids as they got in. "One more day before we head home," Mr. Keller told us. "We'll spend the night at Flagstaff and then we'll leave for Colorado, bright and early."

Danny offered his hand to help me into the bus. "Are you sure you're okay?" he asked, pointing the way to his seat.

I nodded, feeling flutters in my stomach as we sat side by side.

From his backpack, he pulled out a handbook. "You were so interested in the animals back there, I thought you'd like to check this out."

He turned to a picture of a kaibab squirrel. Its

tail was completely white, and the caption said it was rare and endangered and lived only on the North Rim.

"The squirrel I saw had a grey tail with white underneath," I said. "Must not be a kaibab." I paged through his book. "This is really cool."

"It's yours," Danny said, his eyes dancing.

I wondered why he was giving it away. Had he already memorized it?

"Thanks," I said, holding the book, "for this. And for saving my life, uh, back there." I started to feel a bit shy. There wasn't much more to say, so I got up to go. "I better get back to Andie now. See you later."

As I headed down the aisle, Andie shot me her thumbs-up sign. She eyed the book Danny had just given me. "What's that?"

I showed her the animal guidebook. "Isn't it terrific?"

She whistled. "So, tell me everything!" she said as I sat down. "What's going on between you two?"

"How should I know?" I said, puzzled at my own excitement over Danny. "I mean, he's like a big brother. That's all."

"That's *not* all," she insisted. "He kept you from being a skinny little grease spot at the bottom of the Grand Canyon!"

It was hard to keep from grinning.

When we arrived in Flagstaff, Andie and I

settled into our motel room. All of us had supper at a McDonald's nearby, then some kids went swimming while others played Rook on the pool patio.

I searched for a pay phone. It had been days since I talked to Mom. I found a phone in the motel lobby and dialed the operator to call collect.

The baby-sitter answered. It was Marcia Greene, a straight-A student from my school. "Hi, Marcia," I said. "It's Holly. Please take the call."

After the operator was off the line, I asked Marcia, "Where's my mom?"

There was an awkward pause. "Just a minute," she said. "Here's Carrie."

"Hi, Holly," Carrie said when she got on. "Where are you?"

"In Arizona. We'll be home tomorrow night."

"Goody! Can't wait to see you, Holly. It's boring without you."

Carrie's voice made me homesick. "Where's Mom?" I asked.

"Out on a date."

I almost choked. "A date? Who with?"

"Some man," Carrie said.

"Do I know him?" I said, feeling like a parent screening a prospective date.

"I don't think so. His name's Mr. Tate. He's new at church. They went out to dinner somewhere fancy."

I coughed. "How do you know?"

"Well, Mom never dresses up to go to the Golden Arches, does she?"

"I guess you're right," I said, laughing only on the outside. "Tell Mom I called. See you tomorrow night!"

I hung up. What a nightmare! Mom had never loved anyone but Daddy—at least until he got remarried. I thought she was happy being single. Now while I was hundreds of miles away on choir tour she was dating again. Four years since her divorce from Daddy. Why would she want to start dating now?

Slowly I climbed the stairs to our room. Andie was out swimming, so I took a long shower, then climbed into bed without waiting for her.

When my watch beeped out the time at six the next morning, I woke up immediately. My first thought was of Mom. I couldn't wait to get back home . . . where I should've been last night! I was desperate for a heart-to-heart talk with Mom. Where was her good sense?

I leaped out of bed and stuffed my clothes into an overnight bag.

"What's your rush?" Andie said, rubbing her eyes. "You're not homesick, are you?"

"No," I said.

"Hey, what's bugging you?" she asked, sitting up, stretching. "You're always so cheerful in the morning."

"Mom's dating again." I bunched up my pajamas and thrust them deep into the bag.

Andie scrunched her nose. "She's what?"

"You heard me."

"Did I miss something? How do you know she's

dating again?" She took her brush from the nightstand and began counting the strokes out loud. Stopping at fifteen, she said, "Come on, Holly. Talk to me."

I wanted to cry. "I called home last night, and Carrie said Mom was out on a date," I explained. "Out with some guy she met at church, a Mr. Tate." I swallowed hard. "And now I'm just upset with her, that's all."

"How come?" Andie looked puzzled. "You should be happy for her, Holly. Doesn't this mean she's growing—you know, accepting the divorce and all that?"

I shrugged. I didn't think Mom needed to grow. She seemed fine just the way she was.

Andie persisted. "Well, it *is* a good sign, isn't it?"

I didn't want to talk about it. Besides, she had no idea what it was like to lose a father to divorce and possibly a mother to remarriage.

No idea at all.

Carrie and Mom were waiting in the church parking lot when our bus finally rolled into Dressel Hills. It was dark, but in the streetlight I could see a purple and pink balloon bouquet floating up out of the car window. Grinning, Carrie waved it back and forth.

As the bus came to a stop, the kids jumped up and began gathering up small pieces of luggage under the seats.

"Hey, Holly," called Jared, in the middle of the stampede. "Need help?"

"No thanks," I replied. I'd made sure to avoid him ever since my near-death in the Grand Canyon.

Andie poked me. "Are you *sure* you don't want the finest-looking boy in Dressel Hills to help you with your bags?"

"*He* almost got me killed." I stashed the nature book from Danny into my backpack.

"You're guarding that book pretty well, I see," she teased.

"It's full of good stuff," I said.

"Well, if you can't find all the facts in there," she said, tapping the book through the backpack, "I know a guy who's a walking encyclopedia." Andie jerked her head towards Danny, and I blushed.

Loaded down with backpacks, we squeezed through the swarm of kids leaving the bus. At last, we were outside. We gathered around as the driver opened the huge luggage compartment.

My eight-year-old sister jumped out of the car. "Holly!" she cried, running toward me. "Look! I got you these balloons with my own money."

"What a sweetie," I said. "Thanks!"

Surprisingly, Andie's and my suitcases were among the first to be unloaded. Mom had already opened the trunk, and Andie lugged her stuff over to our car while Mom stood smiling. No, grinning.

"Welcome home, Holly-Heart." She hugged me. Maybe my eyes were pulling tricks on me, but Mom looked happier than she had in four years. My stomach tightened. Four years ago Daddy had divorced us—I mean, *her*. What did it mean, this glow on her face?

"How was choir tour?" she asked, arranging my luggage in the trunk.

"Fine," I said.

"Let's hear about Disneyland," she said as

Andie and I climbed into the back seat, the balloons bobbing between us.

Carrie turned around and peered over the front seat. "Did you get me a Mickey Mouse?" she asked.

"Wait and see," I teased her.

I wanted to fire my questions about Mom's new love interest, but I bit my lip instead. I had to wait until Andie and Carrie weren't around.

When we stopped at a red light, Carrie asked, "Did you visit your daddy?"

"He's *your* daddy, too," I said.

"I don't have a daddy."

"What does she mean?" Andie said, looking surprised.

"You do so," I said.

Mom explained. "She doesn't remember her father because she was so young when he left."

"Well?" Carrie wouldn't let it go. "Did you see him?"

"Uh-huh," I said slowly, not wanting to let on how important my visit with him had been.

"What's he li—?"

"Carrie," Mom interrupted. "Maybe Holly doesn't want to discuss it right now."

"It's okay," I said, sticking up for Carrie.

It was obvious it was *Mom* who didn't want to discuss it. Her attitude upset me. So I decided to get right to the heart of things. "I've made a decision," I announced. "I'm going to spend the summer with Daddy."

"You're what?" Carrie hollered.

"Wait a minute, Holly," Mom said. "We haven't talked about any of this yet."

"Yeah," Carrie said. "I won't let you go away all summer."

"Neither will I." Andie glared at me.

Let me? Nobody seemed to care what *I* wanted. Even Andie was close to blowing up over it. Fortunately, we turned into her driveway before she had time to have a hissy fit.

Unloading her stuff, Andie turned to me under the raised trunk. "Oh, Holly," her voice shook. "I can't believe you'd really go and do this."

"What? Like it's some horrible hideous thing to want to get better acquainted with your father?"

"*You* know what I'm talking about," she said in a huff.

It was deathly still as Mom drove the short distance home. But as we turned onto Downhill Court, Mom said, "Holly, I understand Carrie told you that I was away on a date last night. His name is Mike Tate, and he will be meeting us at home."

Tate? That rhymed perfectly with date and late. He wouldn't be Mom's date tonight, or at all, if I hadn't been so late. This mess could've been avoided if I hadn't been off on choir tour.

"He's coming over?" Carrie asked excitedly.

Mom nodded. "Only for a short time. We have something important to discuss. And I'd like him to meet Holly."

"Terrific," I mumbled, wondering how this guy had managed to upstage my return home. This was supposed to be *my* night!

Our headlights bounced off a somber blue car up ahead. "There he is," Carrie said, pointing as we pulled into the driveway.

A stocky man got out of the car and came around to help Mom with her door. It reminded me of Danny offering his hand to help me climb into the bus yesterday.

"Holly," Mom said, "I'd like you to meet Mike Tate. Mike, this is my daughter, Holly."

I shifted the balloon bouquet to my left wrist so I could shake his hand. "Nice to meet you," I mumbled.

"It's nice to meet you, too, Holly," Mr. Tate said. "Your mother has told me a lot about you."

Like what? I wondered. I didn't like the idea of Mom discussing me with some guy she'd just met.

Mr. Tate gathered up my luggage, and we headed for the front door. Under the light of our porch lamp, I saw a shiny bald spot on his head. He opened the screen door, holding it while Mom found her key. I could tell by the way he stood there what type he'd be—polite and structured. He wasn't nearly as tall as Daddy. Or as handsome.

Inside, Mom said, "Holly, why don't you go ahead and unpack? Just throw your dirty clothes in the hamper. I'll do the wash tomorrow night."

I grabbed my bags and headed for the stairs. She sure was in a hurry to get rid of me. When I glanced back, I saw Mr. Tate touch the tip of Mom's elbow, guiding her through the dining room towards the kitchen.

"We'll be in here if you need anything," Mom called.

Carrie asked, "Can I have a bubble bath, Mommy?"

"That's fine," Mom said. "Holly-Heart, could you help Carrie with her hair?"

"Sure, Mom," I said. Carrie and I headed upstairs, leaving Mom and this Mr. Tate person sitting at the bar in our kitchen.

"How much bubble bath can I put in?" Carrie called from the bathroom.

"Doesn't matter," I said, lugging my bags into my room.

"Goody." Carrie ran to the hallway closet and came back with three bottles of the bubble stuff.

"What are you doing?"

She giggled. "You said it didn't matter."

"Just don't flood the bathroom with suds," I said, closing the door.

Back in my room, my stuffed animals stared at me from their shelf-home near my window seat—my favorite place to think. And write.

I yanked my backpack off, pulling out a droopy-eyed stuffed animal. "Welcome back, Bearie-O," I said to the tan teddy bear. He actually belonged to Andie. Six years ago we'd traded favorite bears—a cool thing to do with your best friend.

I sat on my canopy bed and leaned Bearie-O gently against my pillow. "What do *you* think of my summer plans?" I asked the love-worn teddy. He looked intently at me. At least *he* would listen. A good trait for a best friend. Mothers, too.

"I've saved up secret wishes ever since Daddy left," I whispered. "You're the only one who knows them all."

I stroked the place on his head where the fur was sparse, a bald spot made from kissing his teddy head good night. Yikes! It made me think of bald Mr. Tate downstairs with Mom right now!

I reached for the mini straw hat on my Hillbilly Mouse. Plopping it down on Bearie-O, I prayed out loud. "Please, Lord, don't let this man mess up our lives."

I unpacked the Mickey Mouse I'd purchased for Carrie and marched down the hall. "Knock, knock," I said, tapping on the bathroom door.

"Who's there?" Carrie answered, playing along.

"Mickey Mouse."

Carrie squealed, "Really?"

I sneaked Mickey around the door and peeked him in.

More squealing.

"Do you need a shampoo, little girl?" Mickey said in a high-pitched voice.

"Nope, it's all done," Carrie answered.

It was *my* turn to peek around the door. There sat Carrie in a mountain of shampoo bubbles—suds closing in on her eyebrows.

"It's time for some expert help," I said. "Besides, you need to get to bed soon. Tomorrow's Sunday."

"Let Mickey watch us rinse my hair," Carrie said.

"Okay." I set Mickey on the sink counter,

wondering what I was like at eight. I remembered a surprise birthday gift from Daddy—a shiny red bike. But that was all.

"Do you like Mr. Tate?" Carrie asked between rinsings.

"Don't know him," I said.

"He's real nice, Holly. You should see what he got me."

I felt uneasy. Not only was he showering my mother with attention, he was buying off my little sister.

"I'll show you the present when I say my prayers." She held her breath and disappeared under the bubbles. Golden strands of hair floated up like a mermaid's.

At last her bath was done. I used the hair dryer on her waist length locks and braided it damp to keep the tangles out, the way I did my own.

When we got to her room, I was surprised to see a giant mermaid posed on her bed.

"This is new, isn't it?" I asked.

"From Mr. Tate."

"That's nice."

It was. *He* wasn't. I knew I wouldn't let myself like this man. Presents or not, he had no business with our family.

I listened to Carrie say her prayers, then I tucked her in.

"I'm glad you're home again, Holly," said Carrie. "You really won't go off to California this summer, will you?" Her soft brown eyes pleaded with me.

"I want to get to know Daddy better, Carrie. Can you understand that?"

"What about *me*?" She curled her lip into a pout. "What will *I* do all summer?"

"Let's talk about it tomorrow," I said, feeling like a grownup.

"You can talk all you want," she said, "but it won't change my mind. Not one bit!"

I hugged my spunky sis, then left the door cracked open to let the hall light shine in a little. I hurried to my window seat for some secret list-making.

Curling up, I began writing. The left side: reasons for going to California. The right side: reasons for staying home.

CALIFORNIA	**HOME**
1. Get to know Daddy.	1. Keep Mom away from Mr. Tate.
2. Learn more about my childhood from Daddy.	2. Go camping and rafting with Andie and family.
3. Experience the excitement of a beach house setting.	3. Make Carrie happy.
4. Prove to Mom I am grownup enough.	4. Attend youth services and parties.
	5. Find out if Danny Myers really likes me.

So far, staying home had five reasons and going to California only four.

I reached for my teen devotional. After reading it, I wrote #5: *Talk to Daddy about God.*

Now both sides were tied.

The next morning before I got out of bed I wrote in my diary—*Sunday, March 28th*. Then I copied the secret California list into my journal. Afterwards, I prayed.

"Please, oh please, dear Lord, make Mom let me go to visit Daddy this summer. It's the most important thing in my life right now. Honest! Amen."

Feeling satisfied that I was approaching this in a mature Christian manner, I went downstairs and poured myself a bowl of my favorite cereal. After breakfast I called Andie. No answer. She must have gone to early church.

Just as I hung up, the phone rang. I could tell it was long distance by the faraway sound on the line. Daddy!

"How was your trip home?" he asked.

"Perfect," I said.

"The Grand Canyon?"

I remembered the powerful feeling I had there. "I think I know what you mean about that place," I said softly.

"It's amazing," he said. "And Holly, you'd be even more inspired if you ever have the chance to hike down into it."

"I, uh, sort of did that," I said, remembering my near-fatal fall.

"How was it?" he asked.

"Much scarier than I dreamed it would be." I didn't explain what had happened. I didn't want to hear a lecture on safety. Not now.

"Pretty steep, isn't it?" He paused, then asked, "Have you thought any more about your summer plans?"

I wanted to say Mom was chewing her nails over his invitation, but didn't. It could be a mistake to get him in the middle of things here.

"I really want to come—more than anything!" I said, hesitating. "But there's, uh, lots of stuff going on here. I just don't know how it'll go."

"Well, Holly, I can get your plane tickets in a jiffy, that's no problem. Let me know when you're sure. Okay?"

"Okay, Daddy. Thanks."

"How's Carrie?" he asked.

"Spunky as ever," I said, laughing. "She missed me so much, she bought balloons with her own money."

He chuckled. "Tell her thanks for sending the art work. I hung it up on the wall in my study."

"Don't *you* want to tell her?"

"Can't this time. I'm in a rush. Have an appointment with a client in thirty minutes. I'll talk to you soon. Good-bye, Holly."

I hung up feeling a little sad that he was off to work instead of church.

Tiptoeing up the steps, I heard Mom singing. I went to her bedroom door and knocked.

"Come in," she called cheerfully.

As I entered, she drew back the curtains, letting the morning drift in. Dressed in her soft pink robe, Mom looked like an angel, her blonde hair spilling forward on her shoulders. She sat down on the bed.

"Can we talk?" I asked.

She patted the bed beside her. "Sure, what's up?"

"Mr. Tate," I said, getting right to the point.

"Oh?"

"How long have you known him, Mom?"

She looked at the ceiling, like she was counting something invisible. "About ten days, I guess."

"You've got to be kidding," I said. "And you've been out with him? Mom, he could be a bank robber, a murderer, a—"

"Honey," she interrupted. "I met him at *church*."

"I've never seen him there before."

"He transferred from another church. He and his son."

I sighed. "He's been married before?"

"His wife died several years ago. He's very lonely." She touched my hair.

How could I follow up with my anti-Tate campaign when Mom looked so happy? I couldn't tamper with that. At least not now.

"Do you like him?" I asked.

"He's very nice," she said. "And his adorable little boy is in my Sunday school class. *He* introduced me to Mike."

I studied her.

"I hope you'll give him a chance, Holly-Heart, even though it must be difficult for you."

"Okay, I guess." I wanted to ask why he picked our church to transfer to, why he was so bald, and stuff like that. Instead, I hugged her and ran to wake Carrie for Sunday school. Maybe she was right. Maybe I *should* give Mike Tate a chance. But he'd better prove himself fast, because I wasn't going to give him very long.

After school on Monday I was at my locker, dropping off books and loading up my shoulder bag, when Jared popped around my locker door.

"Boo!"

"Eek!" I squealed, jumping back.

"Didn't scare you, did I?"

"Get away from me," I said, wanting to slap him silly.

"Let's go skating next Friday, Holly-Heart."

"Don't call me that," I said coldly.

"Oh, that's right. I forgot," he said. "That name's only for close friends and relatives."

"Perfect, you remembered. Now remember *not* to say it." I glimpsed Andie speeding towards us.

She grabbed my arm. "Quick—let me copy your English homework assignment," she said, out of breath.

"It's here somewhere," I said, flipping through my notebook. "There." I handed it to her, wondering why she hadn't paid attention in Miss Wannamaker's class.

Jared leaned over my shoulder, real close. "Cool handwriting, Holly."

"You need a translator for yours," Andie joked, scribbling the assignment on the back of her lunch bag.

Jared leaned on my locker, almost in it. "That's some ingenious essay Miss W has planned. 'Write about your secret summer fantasy—what you would most like to have happen this summer,'" he said, mimicking Miss W's sweet voice. "Where do you think she gets these wild ideas for our writing assignments?"

"She has a creative mind," I said, gathering my books and slamming my locker.

"When are you going to start writing your essay, Holly? It's due next week," Andie asked.

"I *am* writing it—in my mind."

Finished scribbling, Andie pushed the brown lunch bag into her jeans pocket and together we squeezed through the crowd of kids in the hall.

"Wish I could pull an A on this paper," Andie said.

"I have zillions of ideas," I said, rearranging the books in my arm.

"Oh, yeah? What's *your* summer fantasy?" Jared asked, suddenly behind me.

I ignored him. *Did he ever give up?*

"Come on, Holly," he said. "Forget the past. Let's start over like we'd never met."

Wish that was true, I thought. Up until last winter, not one guy had shown interest in me. I figured it was because I was as flat as Kansas and skinnier than the Oklahoma panhandle. Andie said it was because I was a threat to a guy's I.Q. Mom said it didn't matter, I was too young to care what boys thought. But Jared? Jared had said I was *perfect,* because he liked me just the way I was. The fact that it was only one of his many lines still hurt.

"So Holly, what'll it be?" Jared asked, pressing against the crowd, next to me. "Will you please go skating with me Friday?"

"Leave her alone," Andie snarled. "Can't you understand English?"

Jared whined like a wounded puppy—one of his better routines. He slumped back away from me, and the crowd devoured him. I quickened my pace to match Andie's.

Outside, Andie said, "Just what *is* your secret summer fantasy, Holly?" She shot me a glance.

"You already know," I said. "We've discussed it enough, and I'm not saying more till I know what's really going to happen." I was determined not to tell her I had talked with Daddy yesterday. I didn't want to get into another argument with her.

Andie sulked for a moment. Then she said, "Give me some ideas for English, Holly. What sort of summer fantasy could I possibly write?"

"Here's one," I said. "You're on a wild raft trip, and you fall in love with the cute guide. How's *that* for a summer fantasy?"

"Good deal! You oughta be a writer, you know," Andie said.

"I *am* a writer, just not a published one," I said pushing my hair back over my shoulder. "But someday!"

Outside, we skipped down the steps of Dressel Hills Junior High and headed for Aspen Street, where mobs of ski buffs mingled in the wintertime. Things were much quieter now. Ski resorts had reduced their rates for spring skiing, and guys skied without shirts or with cutoffs, getting a jump on their summer tans.

Andie interrupted my thoughts. "Has Danny called yet?"

"Nope. And he wasn't in church yesterday, either."

"So you were looking for him, weren't you?"

"Not exactly."

"Of course you were, Holly! The guy saved your life, after all!"

I blushed. "Do you really think he likes me?"

"He gave you his guide book, didn't he?" Andie said. "I mean, it's so cool, Holly. After the way

Jared treated you, you deserve this kind of attention. Try to enjoy it!"

"It won't matter when I'm out in California this summer," I said. A California summer would be a great change from this boring town. Sun and fun, and hot breezes blowing in off the ocean. Late nights and long talks with Daddy . . . the way it used to be.

"Oh, no. Not *that* again." Andie rolled her eyes.

I turned away, looking up at the mountains around us. The ski runs, covered with the last snow of winter, soon would be bare and brown. Ski lifts would carry up hikers in shorts and sturdy leather boots instead of skiers in colorful parkas. The countdown to summer vacation had begun!

Halfway to the end of Downhill Court, I saw Mr. Tate's boring blue Ford turn into our driveway.

Andie spotted it, too. "Looks like you've got company."

"It's not *my* company." I wanted to turn and hightail it back to school. Then I heard footsteps behind me.

It was Carrie. A small boy wearing a red baseball cap trailed behind her.

"Hi, Holly. Hi, Andie," Carrie called as she brushed past us.

"What's the rush?" I asked.

"Zachary has to throw up," she shouted over her shoulder. They dashed into the house.

Andie snorted. "Where'd she find *him*?"

I shrugged my shoulders. "Never seen him before in my life," I said, puzzled.

"Isn't he too young to be hanging out with Carrie?" she asked. We climbed the steps leading to our redwood porch.

"Who knows? One thing's for sure, he's new around here." I opened the front door, eager to find out what was going on.

Inside, the house was in an uproar. Mom was standing outside the bathroom door, wringing her hands. Carrie was hanging on her arm, hands over her ears, and Zachary—whoever he was—was in the bathroom, making horrible retching sounds.

"What's going on?" I asked. "Who's Zachary?"

Just then, Mr. Tate emerged from the bathroom with the white-faced boy.

"Er, excuse me," I said, moving out of the way.

Carrie patted the boy on the back. "You okay, Zachary?"

He nodded weakly. He didn't look okay to me.

"Let's find a place for you to rest," Mr. Tate said. Mom led Zachary downstairs to the family room. Mr. Tate followed.

"What's wrong with him?" I whispered to Carrie.

"Some pill he has to take," she said. "Makes him sick."

Then it hit me. Zachary was Mr. Tate's kid!

"What are *they* doing here?" I asked.

"Mr. Tate's cooking lasagna for dinner," Carrie said.

"What?" I was shocked. Men like Mr. Tate seemed too resourceful in my opinion. I didn't care to stick around and eat his meal.

"Can I eat at your house tonight?" I asked Andie, imitating the kid from the stuffing commercial.

"Sure!" Andie said, catching on. "We're having Stovetop Stuffing!" We giggled loudly.

"Holly, stop clowning around and come here!" Mom called from the bottom of the stairs.

I hurried down, embarrassed that she had overheard.

"Please keep the noise down. And get a blanket for Zachary," she said.

"And a pillow," Mr. Tate called.

Feeling like a slave for Mr. Tate's sick kid, I went to the hall linen closet and pulled out blankets and a pillow. Some gall, exposing all of us to the flu! When I came down the stairs, arms loaded, Mom and Mr. Tate were still hovering over Zachary. They didn't even say "Thank you."

Andie and I escaped upstairs to my room. I grabbed my notebook and a pencil.

"What's that for?" Andie asked, flopping onto my bed.

I scribbled off a limerick. "Listen to this," I said, laughing so hard I could barely read.

"There once was a man named Tate
With a balding pate like fish bait.
His son had the flu
He threw up on cue
Such a terrible, horrible fate!"

Andie burst into giggles. "Mr. Tate's head doesn't look *wormy*!"

"But worms *are* smooth and don't have hair," I said.

Andie held her sides, laughing.

"I rest my case," I said as Andie reached for my notebook.

"Here, let's think of all the words that rhyme with Tate," she said.

"Okay, first off—*regurgitate*. It even has Tate at the end!" I scratched my head. "And it describes how I feel about him hanging around here with his throw-uppy kid."

"I know what you mean," Andie said. "If my mother was divorced and Tate was cooking lasagna for us, I'd create a scene and *agitate* him so he'd *irritate* my mother."

I continued. "Then I'd *terminate* their social life and *accentuate* the good life—life before Tate, who's looking for a *mate*."

Andie clapped, and I took a bow. "Hey, you're pretty good yourself. There's hidden literary talent in there," I said, knocking on her curly head.

Andie replied, "I would *hate* to see you *salivate*

on Tate's cooking. Who knows, you might *disintegrate*!"

More giggles.

Andie checked her watch. "Yikes, gotta *terminate* this conversation." She staggered out of my room, giggling uncontrollably.

"You gonna *isolate* me?" I called after her.

She waved, holding her stomach as she left.

I stayed holed up in my room. No need to be around Mr. Tate any more than I had to.

"Holly! Supper's ready!" Mom called.

Great, I thought as I headed downstairs, straight towards Tate's lasagna.

Everyone but Mr. Tate was seated at the dining room table when I arrived. Since my usual place was already taken by Zachary, I started to sit in the seat nearest me—the head of the table, where Daddy had always sat.

Mom stopped me. "Holly, dear," she said. "Could you sit beside Zachary? I was saving that seat for Mike."

Saving Daddy's seat for Mike? I forced myself not to pull a face. Obediently I went to the empty chair next to Zachary and gave him a fakey smile as I sat down.

Mr. Tate came in carrying the lasagna between two hotpads. "I think we're ready to begin," he said, setting the Corningware in the middle of the table. He looked silly standing there wearing Mom's pink-and-white striped "World's Greatest Cook" apron.

Mr. Domesti-tate, I thought, smothering my

snickers. Too bad Andie wasn't here to share my great puns.

Mr. Tate took off the apron and sat down. "Shall we hold hands for prayer?" he asked.

"We usually just fold our hands," I said quickly. I didn't want to hold Zachary's germy little paw. And I didn't want Mr. Tate holding my mom's hand, either!

Mom stared at me, but Mr. Tate said, "All right, let's just fold our hands then." He bowed his head and prayed a long and rumbling prayer, something about "our most merciful, gracious Redeemer" and "thou who hast covered all our iniquities." It didn't sound anything like the way Mom prayed. She talked to Jesus like he was her best friend.

After the prayer, Mr. Tate began dishing out the lasagna. When my turn came, he said, "Pass your plate, Holly." I held out my plate, and he served me a huge piece. I was about to pull it back when he said, "Wait, looks like yours could use a bit more sauce."

Sulking, I waited while my plate got another gooey spoonful. Then I ate slowly, keeping my eyes down so I wouldn't have to talk to anyone. Mom chatted with Zachary, who leaned on her arm, looking pale and tired. Carrie talked to him too, seeming to enjoy the extra mouths at our table.

Not me.

Mr. Tate helped himself to more lasagna. "Well,

Holly, I never heard about your choir tour," he said. "How was it?"

"Fine, thanks," I said. Mom caught my eye. Her face was telegraphing little messages. *Be polite! Say something!*

Mr. Tate buttered his roll. "Where did you go?"

"To California," I said.

"See any interesting sights?" he asked, taking a bite.

"I saw my dad," I said.

Dead silence. I didn't dare look at Mom. "That's nice," Mr. Tate said at last.

"And we went to Disneyland and then to the south rim of the Grand Canyon."

He cleared his throat. "I prefer God's creation to man's, don't you? The Grand Canyon is so much more inspiring than anything human beings could ever create."

"I guess so." I didn't dare say that I thought Disneyland was just as cool as the Grand Canyon—man-made or not!

Mr. Tate changed the subject. "How do you like the lasagna, Holly?" he asked as I scraped up the last bite on my plate.

I wanted to be flippant and say something like, "Well, I'm eating it, aren't I?" Instead I nodded my head and forced a smile since my mouth was full of his cooking.

"She's trying to be polite," Mom said *for me*. "When her mouth is empty she'll tell you what she thinks of this recipe, won't you, Holly?"

Inside, I churned with anger. Couldn't they all

just leave me alone? I held a napkin over my mouth, making it obvious to everyone I was in the process of chewing . . . not talking. No way would I compliment Mr. Tate on his cooking ability. He might get the wrong idea and decide to treat us to his food—and his presence—more often.

"Daddy," Zachary whined, "I don't feel well."

"I'll take care of him, Mike," Mom said. "Go ahead and finish your meal." She led Zachary down the stairs to the family room.

Carrie finished her supper and went downstairs to talk to Zachary, while Mom and Mr. Tate moved into the living room to drink their tea. Naturally, I got stuck cleaning up. I cleared the table, then I stacked the dishes in the dishwasher. Evidently The Cook was not ready to demonstrate his domestic skills in the area of kitchen duty. It appeared that he'd used every pot and pan in the entire house. Scrubbing them would give me time to think. And to eavesdrop on the cozy little conversation down the hall!

Slopping around in the dish suds, I thought about that disgusting little Zachary Tate. He'd leaned on Mom all during supper, whining. And sneezed his germs all over us! I've heard that an only child can be a real pain, getting all the attention and stuff, but this was ridiculous. Even Carrie got sucked into catering to him.

Maybe I could try to ignore the whole thing. Maybe Mom would soon get sick of having zillions of extra people around. But by the frequency of her smiles, who was to say what would happen?

Wiping off the table, I heard laughter. It was Mom. Slowly, with dripping hands, I peeked around the doorway.

Gulp!

Mr. Tate's arm was resting on the back of the sofa. Behind my mother! And it looked like he was moving in for the kill!

I closed my eyes. *Please God. Do something quick!* I imagined a lightning bolt descending from heaven, ripping through the roof, and frying the spot between Mr. Tate and Mom. Closest to Mr. Tate's side, of course.

Right then Carrie screamed from the family room. "Quick! Something's wrong with Zachary!"

Mom jumped to her feet, following Mr. Tate down to the family room. The timing was miraculous. *Thanks, God, you did it!*

I ran to see what could possibly be wrong with Mr. Tate's spoiled brat.

I sat at the top of the family room steps observing the situation. What *was* wrong with Zachary?

"Call the hospital!" Mr. Tate said to Mom. She snatched up the cordless phone, punching the numbers as fast as she could. Carrie looked on fearfully as Mr. Tate carried Zach to the couch. He felt his face, then took his pulse. Zachary's face was a chalky white.

I inched my way down the stairs, now sitting at the bottom. The minute Mom was off the phone I asked, "What's wrong?"

Mom ignored my question. Instead, she hurried to Zach's side. "The doctor wants to see him, Mike." She stroked Zach's head.

In one swift move, Mr. Tate picked Zach up,

blanket and all. I moved aside as they rushed past me up the steps. Carrie and I followed them to the living room.

Mom stood in the doorway peering out as Mr. Tate put his kid in the car. "I wonder if I shouldn't follow them down to the hospital," she said, thinking out loud.

"I wanna go too," Carrie pleaded.

"All right, get your jacket. Hurry!" Mom flew to her room to get her coat and purse.

Seconds later the back door banged behind them, and suddenly the house was silent.

I stood alone in the kitchen. "Mr. bald Michael Tate—dissipate . . . evaporate!" I said out loud. I giggled uncontrollaby. Then I made up another rhyme.

"1-3-5, 4-6-8
Dirty dishes, you can wait.
Peace and quiet, no Mike Tate—
Yes! It's time to celebrate!"

I ran to the freezer and pulled out a carton of strawberry ice cream. Hurrah for flu bugs, the nasty little things! They weren't all bad—they had their up side, too. Like keeping certain people apart. "Mom and Tate—please separate!" I said out loud.

If Zach was as sick as he looked, no chance would Mom be dating Mr. Tate for at least a week! I didn't need a degree in medicine to see that *this* was no twenty-four hour flu. With Mr. Tate out of the picture that long, I'd have time to work on

Mom. Getting her to say yes to the California visit was my top priority.

Halfway through my ice cream binge, the phone rang.

"Hello?" I said.

"Holly?" *It was Danny Myers!* "Are you going to the skating party on Friday?" he asked. Almost shyly.

"Uh, yes, I'm going," I said, excited.

"Great. Then I'll see you there, okay?" he said. "Catch you later, Holly. Bye."

Just like that, he hung up. I stood staring at the phone. I wondered if he'd hung up like this with his old girlfriend, Alissa. She'd moved away a month before choir tour—lucky for me. Last I heard, Danny wrote her letters occasionally. But they were just friends now.

I reached for the phone to call Andie. "Guess what?" I said when she answered.

"Hmm, let's see," she said.

"C'mon, Andie. Guess!"

"You're back with Jared?" she teased.

"Get it right . . . it's something fabulous."

"Yes!" she shouted into the phone. "Danny called, right?"

"He called about Friday night," I said.

"Did he ask you out?"

"Not really. But he asked if I was going to the skating party."

"So it's not like a date."

"Mom wouldn't let me even if it was," I said. "I have to be fifteen before I can go on a real date."

"I know. Me, too," said Andie. "Unless someone extra special comes along, then I can crash the dating scene early."

"*My* mother will never change her mind."

"She might approve of Danny Myers, if she met *him*," Andie said. "Get her to drive us Friday night. You could introduce him then."

I twisted my hair. "If Zachary Tate gets over the flu by then, she'll probably have her own date."

"Something Jared won't have," Andie said, snickering. "He's stuck. Can't get anyone to go out with him."

"Thanks to us." I felt proud protecting the rest of the Dressel Hills female population from the likes of two-timing Wilkins. "As Grandma Meredith would say, 'He's cooked his goose.'"

"That's for sure!" Andie agreed.

After we hung up, I went downstairs to read a new mystery I'd borrowed from the school library. An hour and a half later, Mom and Carrie arrived home. Carrie looked worried. Mom looked exhausted.

"How's Zachary?" I asked.

"He's hanging tough," Mom said, tossing her purse onto the bar. "They'll keep him for a couple days while the doctors try out some new medication." Before I could ask what was wrong with him, Mom turned and headed for the stairs. Guess she didn't want to talk much about Zachary—at least not tonight.

♥ ♥ ♥

On Tuesday after school, I confronted Mom about my California trip.

"Holly, you're beginning to bug me about this," she said. She was sitting at the dining room table, sipping her peppermint tea, trying to unwind. "Let's talk about it later, okay?"

When later came—two hours later—I asked her again. We were having supper, minus Mr. Tate.

"Holly, I'm not interested in having this conversation," Mom said.

"But you said we'd talk later," I whined. "Why don't you want to discuss this? It's important to me, Mom."

She sighed. "Your father's lifestyle is much different from ours, Holly."

"How do you know?" I put my fork down, eager for an answer.

"Your grandma Meredith keeps in touch with him. She's told me she's concerned that he's not a Christian."

"Well, so am I, but I don't see why I can't go visit him just because of that."

Mom narrowed her eyes. "Los Angeles isn't exactly the best place for a young girl to spend the summer."

"I won't *be* in L.A. Daddy's house is on the beach—west of there."

"Well, blame it on the beach crowd then," she said as she reached for the basket of rolls. "Your father will be gone to work most of the time. Who knows what might happen?"

"You don't trust me, is that it?"

"Why don't you do something for me, Holly?" she said, buttering her roll. "Think about your decision for the next month or so. Maybe by then you'll feel differently about it."

Change my mind? She had to be kidding!

"Aren't you just hoping I'll forget about this visit?" I said.

"Of course not, Holly." But she avoided meeting my eyes and started fussing over Carrie not having had enough to eat.

"Uh-huh," I muttered. "Right."

Mom was wrong to put me off this way. It was a lousy scheme to delay this all-important decision. A month or so, she said? Well, in thirty days I'd be back with zillions of reasons why I should go!

Wednesday night, Andie and I did homework at *her* house. Andie called it the great Tate-break even though Mr. Tate was at his own house taking care of Zachary. He was on some new medicine. Maybe he was allergic to penicillin, like Andie's little brothers. Mom didn't tell me much about it. We had sort of an unspoken pact going: she wouldn't talk about Mr. Tate and Zachary around me, and I wouldn't talk about Dad and going to California around her.

At Andie's, I helped her with plot ideas for the creative writing assignment in English. She decided to go with my suggestion: the raft trip. While she started her first draft, I multiplied twenty-four hours times the days remaining till Friday. Skate night!

Thursday after school, Jared was still scrounging for a date for the skating party. Poor, pitiful thing!

Andie baited him. "What about asking the Miller twins? You *do* know Paula and Kayla, don't you?"

Jared's eyes lit up.

"They moved here from Philadelphia, same place my uncle and cousins live," I said.

"I heard their dad was stressed out back East and quit his executive job," Andie added.

"That's right," I said. "Uncle Jack suggested they move to our peaceful, stress-free ski village."

"How old are these girls?" Jared asked.

"They're in eighth grade," I said. "Think they'd want to hang around a lowly sevey like you?"

Jared leaned on my locker. "I could make them forget that fact," he said, grinning.

"Fat chance," Andie said.

"So which one of you wants to introduce me?" he asked.

Andie whispered behind my locker door, "He doesn't have a chance! I already filled them in on him."

"Andie, you're wicked," I said, straightening the books in my locker.

"Says who?" She slammed her locker shut.

Jared shifted his books. "Girls, I'm waiting."

"Give up," Andie said. "You're on your own." We turned away, leaving Jared in the dust.

At last, Friday night arrived.

We met at the church and divided up for transportation. Danny rode to the skating rink with the youth pastor in one of the church vans. Jared, Billy Hill—from school—and four other guys rode along. Andie and I rode with her dad.

Inside the skating rink, Danny waited for me near the pop machine.

"Soda?" he asked, pulling some change out of his black jeans.

"Sure." I watched as he selected my favorite soda pop. His light green sweatshirt was perfect. Made the green in his eyes sparkle.

While I picked out my ice skates, Danny grabbed his and laced them up. Then he helped with my left foot, which wouldn't budge. Stuck on the way into the skate. It would have been embarrassing with any other guy. Not with Danny.

The music swelled as we stepped onto the ice. The rink was crowded. Beginners claimed the middle areas, while speed skaters and show-offs zipped past us on the outer rink.

Danny reached for my hand as we circled the ice. "You're good," he said, smiling down into my eyes.

"Thanks." Butterflies swirled inside me.

After three more times around, Andie grabbed my free hand and called for the others to crack the whip. We got real rowdy then, especially the second time with short little Andie at the tail end. Hanging on for dear life, she flew across the ice, screaming at the top of her lungs.

Soon the other church kids crowded in, and the guys speed skated together. Andie and I stayed with the girls, but secretly, I watched Danny. His long legs made swift, sure strokes on the ice. Some of the other guys were more reckless and crazy, but he was always in control. And fast! He seemed to pass the other guys without even trying.

Andie went off with Billy Hill, and I circled the ice a few times with the girls. Then the loudspeaker crackled. "Couples only," it announced.

Out of nowhere, Jared zoomed up behind me. Before I knew it, he was whirling me towards center ice.

"Let go of me!" I demanded, pushing away from him. I skated toward the snack bar to catch my breath.

Jared followed. "You're great, Holly. Let's try it again," he said, bowing low like a bullfighter ready for the fight.

"Once was too much," I said, turning to look for Danny. Had he missed Jared's skating stunt? I hoped so!

Andie was eating ice cream with Billy Hill. They waved me over to their table. Uninvited, Jared tagged along.

"Lookin' good out there," Billy said, fumbling for an extra chair.

"Thanks." I glanced at Jared. "Wasn't *my* idea."

Andie held her cone up for me to lick.

"Good you came, Billy," Jared said.

He nodded. "Danny's been asking me for about a year. Thought I'd give it a try."

"You'll like our group," I said.

Should've known Billy was Danny's guest.

Perfectly wonderful Danny. Witnessing, praying in public, making all the right moves.

Andie bit into her cone, staring at Jared like he wasn't welcome. "That was some sneaky action out there on the ice," she sneered.

"Are you Holly's bodyguard or what?" Jared snapped back. Billy looked uncomfortable. Jared glared at Andie. Then he got up and went to the snack counter.

"Want to help teach Billy how to skate?" Andie asked, obviously glad to see Jared gone.

I smiled. "You're kidding, right?"

"Nope," Billy said. "It's my first time."

"You're fabulous on the basketball court," I said, meaning it. "There's no way you'll have trouble skating."

"Hey, how can I go wrong with the two of you teaching me?" he replied.

We headed for the ice, laughing as we went. Halfway around, Billy took off skating by himself.

"Would you look at that?" Andie said. "He doesn't need our help."

"Maybe not on the ice," I said.

"You're right," Andie said. "Might feel strange being the only kid in the group . . . who's not a Christian."

She had a point. "Wait for me," I said, skating with her.

"Holly!" I turned to see Danny coming at full speed. He skidded to a stop.

"Want to skate?" he asked.

I stretched my left hand out to meet his, as his

right hand reached around my waist, supporting me as I glided forward. My gloved hand fit safely in his. Sailing on ice with Danny, I was oblivious to the flurry of activity around me. We slowed to a comfortable pace, our legs pushing off to the same rhythm. I couldn't believe this was me—Holly Meredith—skating around the rink with Danny Myers. I wanted this moment to last forever.

Then the music stopped.

"Are you hungry?" Danny asked.

"Are you?"

"Let's grab something," he said.

He ordered two hotdogs, chips, and Coke. Then he paid, like a real date. Or was this his big brother routine again?

We found a table for two. I was so excited sitting here with him, I worried that he could hear my heart pounding.

"Mustard?" he asked.

I nodded. "Thanks."

"Chips?"

"Sure, thanks," I said, feeling bashful.

He opened the mini-bag and we shared them. Twice our fingers touched. Electricity!

Things were weird all of the sudden. During choir tour, we could talk about almost anything. Now, all I could do was mumble stupid stuff about relishes and hot dogs.

"Something bothering you, Holly?" he asked.

"Why?" I asked sheepishly.

"You seem quiet tonight."

I looked into Danny's face. It seemed sincere.

When he smiled, I knew suddenly that I could trust him.

I sighed. "I've been thinking about my mom lately. She's starting to date again, and it bugs me."

"I *thought* there was something wrong," he said, picking up another chip.

"There's more," I said.

"Yeah?"

"Mom won't let me go to California this summer to see my dad," I said.

"Why not?"

"She doesn't approve of Dad's lifestyle. He's not a Christian, you know."

Danny took a swig of pop. "If you go for a couple weeks, what could that hurt?" he said. "Can you convince her that she doesn't have to worry about you?"

"Maybe, but Mom has this idea that California is a thrill-a-minute place and that it'll spoil me." I paused. "Or maybe it's Daddy who will spoil me."

Danny looked at me. "What do *you* think, Holly?"

"All I know is that I'm dying to get to know my father better, that's all."

"Then that should be enough for your mom, too," he said.

Funny, I thought so, too! I smiled at him. It was nice having Danny Myers on my side—even though it wouldn't help convince my mom to let me go. At least it showed me I wasn't so off base after all.

Danny crinkled up his hotdog wrapping and aimed at the trashcan. Bullseye! "Ready to skate again?" he asked, grinning at me.

I returned his smile. "Definitely!"

Slowly, April blossomed into May, and my focus was Danny. I saw him at church on Sundays and at youth service on Tuesday nights. Sometimes he'd show up at my locker and ask if I needed any help on my homework. I wished the work *was* too hard so I could ask for his help. But it wasn't, and I didn't.

Andie was so sure Danny liked me she was holding it over my head. Leverage, she said, for keeping me around all summer. What she didn't know was I intended to go to California no matter what.

Mr. Tate was still showing up at our house. Fixing, repairing, sometimes cooking. Always hovering. Zachary came too. Mom never said anything about why he was still throwing up. Or why she put up with it. Personally, I'd never heard of the flu lasting *this* long!

The last weeks of May inched towards summer like an old tortoise. And California called to me every waking minute. Carrie was beginning to bug me with her crying spells every time I even mentioned California.

Then there was Mom. "I haven't decided yet," she said when I tried to bring up the subject. Even though it looked pretty hopeless, I refused to give up.

Finally, it was Friday, May 28—the last day of school! I was cleaning out my locker when Danny stopped by.

"Did you pack up your smile?" he asked, eyeing a box filled with my junk. I was throwing things in, helter skelter.

"No," I said shortly. But I didn't smile.

"What's wrong?" he asked.

I explained my problem. "Mom still won't talk about California. I'm afraid if I keep bugging her, she'll say no."

"Try looking at it *her* way. Dressel Hills isn't exactly the best place to prepare for big city life, you know," Danny said, laughing. "Who knows what evils may be lurking in L.A."

"Don't make jokes about this," I said. "I'm serious. There's so much I don't know about Daddy. I don't want to wait forever to see him again."

"Do you ever pray about it?" Danny asked, taking the serious approach now.

"Every single day," I said, thinking of my secret list of prayers. Danny Myers was on it, too. Not for the same reason as Daddy, though.

Danny picked up my box of things, and we strolled down the deserted hallway. The Miller twins waved at us from the drinking fountain. They wanted to talk—to Danny. They had been in his Algebra II class last semester.

"What's going on this summer with the youth group?" Kayla asked Danny, ignoring me.

"You're coming on the gondola ride up Copper Mountain, aren't you?" Danny said. "It's tomorrow." He started explaining it to them.

"Psst!" It was Andie sneaking up behind me. Pulling me away from Danny, she whispered, "Look what's happening here. Still want to chance being gone this summer?"

"Danny's not a flirt like Jared," I said.

"Oh, but Danny doesn't have to flirt, now does he?" she said. "*They're* doing all of it."

I watched the brown-eyed beauties. My box of junk was tottering under Danny's arm. Their conversation *was* lasting longer than I cared to admit.

Danny called to me. "Holly, you know Paula and Kayla, don't you?" he asked. "They moved here from Philadelphia last month."

"Yes, we've met. Their dad used to work in the same company as my Uncle Jack." I mustered up a smile.

Kayla said to Danny, "Her Uncle Jack was the one who told our dad about Dressel Hills." She turned to me. "Did you know my dad's trying to get him to move out here—away from the rat race?"

"That'll be the day," I said, wishing my uncle and cousins *did* live closer.

"Well, have a good summer," Paula said.

"See you at the sky ride tomorrow," Kayla said to us. Both twins waved good-bye to Andie and me, then grinned at Danny. He and I turned and headed towards the door, while Andie walked a few feet behind.

Outdoors, Andie waited beside the bike racks while Danny and I talked about tomorrow's gondola ride up Copper Mountain.

"It'll be fun," Danny said. "Maybe we could get a gondola together."

Before I could say anything, he looked at his watch. "Gotta get going," he said. "See you tomorrow."

"Bye." I waved. He headed down the tree-lined street, and I wanted to dance for joy. So much for Paula and Kayla. *I* was the one he wanted to ride up the mountain with!

Andie came up. "What was that all about?" she asked.

"Nothing," I said airily. I glanced back at Danny. He was nearly at the end of the street. From this angle, he practically looked like a grownup. Acted grownup, too. Never acted weird, or embarrassed anyone. Danny was one of those super mature guys every girl dreams of being with.

But I was only thirteen. And even though Andie and I bordered on maturity, every now and then it was fun to act like ten-year-olds. So . . . we skipped all the way to the library.

Inside, we almost bumped into Billy Hill. He was piled high with books.

"Whatcha' doing?" Andie asked.

"Reading some books Danny gave me."

"Like what?" I asked.

He held up one. It was about being a Christian without being weird.

"Looks good," I said.

"Danny liked it. What do *you* think?" he asked Andie.

"Hey, Danny should know. He's the preacher," Andie said.

I didn't like the tone of her voice. It was like she was putting him down or something.

"Danny's not a preacher," I said. "He just knows the Bible better than anyone. And he's not embarrassed to talk about God."

"You got that right," Billy said, heading for the street.

Watching Billy leave, I felt proud to be Danny's friend. If he could get through to Billy Hill, maybe he could give me some pointers about witnessing. I would need them this summer when I talked to Daddy about the Lord. *If* I could ever get Mom to say yes about the trip.

At home I wrote a note and posted it on the refrigerator. *Mom—can we talk some time? Holly.* Mom had no other choice but to see it there.

Strange—making an appointment with my own mother. Not the way it used to be. Before Tate.

Upstairs, I spied on Carrie. She was supposed to be cleaning the junk out from under her bed. Instead, she sat in the middle of the floor, inspecting each item before tossing it in the trash or another pile on the floor.

"Hi," I said, pushing the door open wider. "Some girls at school said their dad is trying to talk Uncle Jack and the cousins into moving out here. Wouldn't it be fun?"

"Mom said they might be," she answered.

"When was *this* discussed?"

Carrie said, "It *wasn't* discussed. Not really."

"So how do you know?"

"Grandma Meredith called when you were gone. She's been calling Mom a lot."

"Really?" I sat down next to her on the floor. "I wonder why."

"I think she's trying to talk Mom into letting you go to California this summer."

I was overjoyed. Someone was finally on *my* side!

"That's perfect," I said. "She knows how much I miss Daddy."

She did, too. Grandpa and Grandma Meredith had stuck by us even though Daddy was their son. They never seemed to be able to put the divorce behind them. Said we were their granddaughters, no matter what.

"Does your daddy know how much you miss him?" Carrie asked. Her voice sounded strange.

I cringed inside. "He's *your* daddy, too, Carrie."
"But I like Mr. Tate better."
"That's only because you hardly know Daddy," I said.
"You don't either," she shot back, "or else you wouldn't be going out there this summer."
"This summer's my business."
Carrie jabbered on. "You'll miss Uncle Jack and our cousins this summer. You'll miss all the fun with Stan and Stephie. Phil and Mark might get into your secret notebooks, and—"
"Stop it, Carrie. You're making me mad."
"I'm mad, too, Holly. I don't want you to go to California. I don't know why Grandma wants you to. She must not be thinking right anymore."
"Watch what you're saying, Carrie."
She kept it up. "She's going to be seventy soon. Old people can't think that good. I'm a kid. Listen to *me*, Holly."
"I've decided, Carrie. That's the way it is. Daddy should be mailing a ticket any day now," I said. I wasn't going to let her beat me with her Miss Know-it-all fit. Besides, saying it might help make it come true.
"Holly-Heart!" Mom was home from work.
I raced to the kitchen where she stood with my note in her hand.
"We'll have to talk fast," she said. "I have to go out."
"Again?" I wailed.
"Holly, please stop these outbursts." She opened the freezer and pulled out pizzas.

"I'm tired of frozen dinners. I want my mother back," I whined.

"I think you're blowing things out of proportion," she said, sitting down. "But, if that's how you feel, we'd *better* talk."

I sat on a bar stool and fiddled with the placemats while I talked. "First of all, Mom, you probably won't believe it, but I've been praying about this summer. A lot." I paused to check her reaction. I could usually tell by her eyes. Nope, they weren't all squinty yet. *Breathe, Holly, breathe,* I told myself.

I continued. "I've been praying that God would help you see how important it is for me to go to California, since it's the most important thing in my life."

She stared at me. No comment. No squinting.

"Do my feelings count?" I asked bravely.

"You bet they do," Mom said.

"Then it's time I visit the other part of my family."

I could see the *family* word bugged her. The eye squinting started.

I took a deep breath. "I feel all torn apart."

"You're right, Holly," Mom said. "An important part of our family *is* missing and has been for a long time."

"But he's still in *my* family," I argued.

"Holly, please don't make this so difficult," she said, her voice trembling.

I brought up the other forbidden topic. "Are you and Mr. Tate . . . ?" I couldn't finish.

She brushed a crumb off the bar. "Perhaps. In time."

"Are you *serious*?"

She nodded. "I would like to get married again someday, Holly . . . to the right man, of course."

My heart sank. "You're kidding! Please say you are! I mean, it's taken this long to get used to Daddy being gone, and—"

"Holly, settle down. I'm not getting married next week. I promise you." She slid off the bar stool and went to the refrigerator.

"Good," I said, hoping Mr. Tate and Mom would break up—soon.

While Mom cut into an apple I returned to the subject of the summer visit.

"Mom, I know you don't approve of my summer plan, but it's right, I know it. I'm a good kid. You don't have to worry about me linking up with the wrong crowd out there. Beach parties don't excite me. Getting to know Daddy does."

Mom's eyes looked serious. I could see she was beginning to understand. Finally, she was listening with her heart.

"And there's another reason," I said softly.

She tilted her head, encouraging me to go on.

"I want to talk to Daddy about the Lord." Silently, I waited for her to say I could go. A yes was on the tip of her tongue. I was sure of it!

Then the phone rang. She ran to get it, the way I do when I think it's a guy. "Hello?" I heard her say. "Hi, Mike."

What timing! Mr. Tate's call had pre-empted me.

I ripped the plastic off the pizzas and threw them in the oven. I set the timer, then stormed upstairs.

Carrie met me in the hallway. "Did you have a fight with Mommy?"

"Never mind," I said.

"You gonna baby-sit me tonight?" she asked.

"You guessed it." I closed my bedroom door. Not a single second of peace passed before Carrie was pounding on my door.

"What now?" I opened the door a crack.

Tears spilled down her cheeks.

"Aw, Carrie, what's wrong?" I reached for her and gave her a big hug. She sobbed something into my chest. Something like if I was far away in California right now, she'd be stuck with Marcia Greene or somebody else for a baby-sitter.

True. But it was Mom's responsibility to look after Carrie, not mine. Carrie's fears were growing, and something had to change that. I thought about it. If Mr. Tate were out of the picture, we'd have Mom back. And I could go to California without worrying about Carrie.

There was one problem, though. Mom's happiness. It could disappear right along with this man . . . and Zachary!

Wiping my sister's tear-streaked face, I pulled my box of school stuff closer. "Wanna help me sort through these papers from my locker?"

We sat on the floor, and I started digging through the box. It was full of important stuff. Like notes passed to me in boring history class. And other things, too. Like the English assignment titled, "My Secret Summer Dream Fantasy." It was squashed down under the end-of-the-year quizzes in math and science.

"What's that?" Carrie asked, as I flipped through the pages of my essay.

"The best English assignment I ever wrote," I said, showing off the A minus. "It was perfectly fabulous. About my secret summer dreams."

"Read it to me," Carrie begged, her nose still stuffy from crying.

"You sure you want to hear it?" I asked.

"Uh huh." She nodded.

"Okay, but you have to promise never to tell anyone about this. Okay?"

"Cross my heart and hope to die, stick a needle in my eye."

"That's gross," I said. "You don't have to say that stuff." Eight-year-olds were far from cool.

I began reading:

"'My Secret Summer Dream Fantasy, by Holly Meredith. The dearest wish that ever could be is to spend the summer of my thirteenth year with my father who lives in California near the Pacific Ocean in a house made of mostly glass windows, especially on the side facing the ocean.'"

What a long sentence! I thought. *Why didn't Miss Wannamaker take points off for that?*

I continued. "'Leaving Dressel Hills, Colorado, behind will be a torturous thing for me, though. My best friend, Andie Martinez, and her family will go without me on their regular camping trip. And this year, an added feature to the normal adventure is a whitewater raft trip down the mighty Arkansas River. I will sacrifice the time of my life in order to get to know the father who left me four years ago when I was just a kid.

"'Then there is my little sister, Carrie, who I must leave behind to face the trials of our mother's momentary fascination with a certain man. Her interest is such that she chooses to spend time with him, much to the dismay of her household, namely her two daughters, and one cat named Goofey.'"

Carrie interrupted. "Goofey doesn't care about anything, Holly. He just eats and sleeps. That's all."

Carrie was right. The cat hadn't been affected by Mom's strange behavior.

I turned the page. "'There is another certain person who is difficult to leave behind. He is the kindest, smartest, coolest best friend a girl could have. He has a photographic memory so all the important things like my favorite cookies and soda pops are right there on the tip of his tongue. Nature and strange animals interest him. His love for God makes me want to talk to the Lord more, the way he does. I can't reveal his name here, but the most fabulous thing that could happen if I get my summer dream-come-true is that he'll agree to do something very weird. This is it: When I leave Dressel Hills for the summer, this special person will promise to read the same books I read while I'm in California. It will be a token of our special friendship. Our reading list will be five books he picks and five I pick.'"

"Wow," said Carrie. "That's ten books. That's a lot!"

"I know," I said, "but listen to what happens next: 'We'd make a reading schedule so that, even though we're hundreds of miles apart, we'd be thinking about the exact same things, precisely at the same time, and we'd be closer to each other for having made this pact.'"

Carrie had more ideas. "Would you seal it with a kiss behind the library?"

"No, silly." Little kids seemed to think that all boyfriends and girlfriends did was kiss. "We're good friends," I explained.

She giggled and snuggled up to me, anxious for more.

I kept reading. "'But the very best and most secret summer fantasy is this: Spending time getting to know my father. And hoping that when he gets to know me better, he'll love me as much as I remember loving him.'"

Carrie was stone still.

"Now you know why it's so important for me to go away." I tucked the English assignment away in my bottom dresser drawer.

Slowly Carrie spoke, "I wish I could say the same thing about our daddy."

It was the first time she'd claimed him as ours. Hers.

"Someday you will," I said, leading her downstairs just as the timer buzzed for the pizza.

She pulled at my hand. "Want some advice?"

"Sure," I said.

"Let Mom read your fantasy story."

Carrie was way off on that idea. Besides, Mom wouldn't appreciate what I'd written about *her*.

"You always let her read your stories and stuff," Carrie said.

Not always, I thought. There were secret lists and secret journals. Secret prayer lists and . . . secret *secrets*.

♥ ♥ ♥

When Mr. Tate arrived for his date with Mom, he looked exhausted. Worried.

Mom came downstairs, wearing her light blue shirtwaist dress. She looked pretty, but preoccupied.

"We'll be attending a meeting at the hospital tonight," Mom informed me, "in case you need to call for any reason." Her words sounded stiff.

Carrie ran to hug her good-bye. I wanted to do the same. But as I crossed the room towards her, Mr. Tate said, "Holly, could you please watch Zachary while we're gone? It'll only be about two hours."

A totally outrageous request. He should've called hours ago. I wanted to say no, but Mom's eyes were squinting almost all the way shut. Something was wrong. I could feel it.

"Next time could you call me ahead of time, please?" I said coldly. Inside I felt like screaming at him. How dare he take my mother and leave me with his spoiled vomity kid!

Mr. Tate ignored my request, handing me a bottle of pills. "Zach will need one of these, thirty minutes from now."

"Do they make him throw up?" Carrie asked as I squeezed the bottle in my hand.

Leave it to Carrie.

I fumed while Mr. Tate explained, "He's fairly nauseous all the time, but that can't be helped. Not immediately. We trust he's improving."

He turned and headed for the car, helping Zachary into the house. Sitting beside him on the sofa, Mr. Tate leaned over and kissed his son. Zachary reached his skinny arms up to his dad and hugged him limply.

"I'll be back soon, son," Mr. Tate said.

Zachary held his thumbs up, just like Andie

always did. Seeing him, Mom made some high-pitched sobbing sounds and rushed out the door.

Mr. Tate kept talking as though nothing had happened. "Zachary should be fine. Just keep him quiet, Holly. No excitement, please." He glanced out the window at Mom, who appeared to have lost it for some unknown reason.

"How am I supposed to do that, when it's impossible to know what's going to happen next around here?" I said, stuffing the pills in my pocket.

Mr. Tate glared back at me. "Don't do this now," he said.

"Do what?" I said, my teeth clenched.

"You know what I mean, Holly," he said so sternly I was immediately convinced to cool it.

I hurried outside to Mom. "Are you okay?"

She dabbed at her eyes and shook her head.

"Mom?" I held her hand. "What's wrong?"

She could only cry.

Mr. Tate came then. He put his arm around her shoulder. "It's about Zachary," he said. "We hope and pray this medication will help him."

Carrie squeezed in between Mom and Mr. Tate, hugging them both.

Mr. Tate studied me with his beady eyes. "We're going to hear a specialist discuss Zachary's illness. It won't be late, Holly," he said.

Zillions of questions zigzagged back and forth in my brain. When Mom and Mr. Tate turned to go, I wanted to shout them out, one by one. Most of all: What about Mom? What was making *her* cry?

Carrie waved as they backed out of the driveway. Then we hurried inside to find Zachary leaning against the green plaid throw pillows on the sofa, sound asleep.

"Are you gonna wake him up for his pill when it's time?" Carrie asked.

"Guess so. Must be pretty powerful stuff to make him so sick," I said, trying to read the label. "What's methotrexate?"

"Never heard of it," Carrie said. She raced to the stairs.

"Where are you going?" I called after her.

In a flash, she came downstairs with a huge book. "Here, Mommy reads out of this."

It was an important-looking medical book. "Where'd you get this?" I asked, touching the tan hardcover.

"Mommy had it in her room this morning. I heard her praying, so I sneaked into the hall to see. She was sitting on the bed, holding it."

I looked in the index under the M's. There it was—methotrexate. A drug prescribed in the maintenance therapy of . . .

I held my breath. Zachary had cancer!

TEN

Slowly, I closed the book and handed it back to Carrie. "Put it where you found it," I said.

"What is it?" Carrie asked. "What's wrong?"

"I'll tell you later. I promise." I hoped she wouldn't bug me about it in front of Zach. He looked wiped out from exhaustion. I could tell by the way his arm was flung off to the side.

Gently untying his Nikes, I pulled them off. I was surprised by the lightness of his body as I lifted his legs onto the sofa. His red baseball cap slipped off to the side as he moved in his sleep. He was mostly bald underneath. No wonder he wore the cap everywhere.

All at once, I felt dreadfully wicked. Here was a very sick boy—not a spoiled brat—who hung all over his dad at mealtime. Who raced to the bathroom for vomiting sessions. Who'd lost all his hair to some powerful drug that was doing damage to his body while attempting to save his life. No wonder my mother sobbed when Zach gave his thumbs-up sign. No wonder!

"Stay here with Zach, will you?" I said to Carrie. Tears blinded my eyes. I ran upstairs to my room and threw myself on my knees. How could God forgive my selfishness? I cried out for forgiveness.

"Have mercy on me, O God, according to your unfailing love; according to your great compassion blot out my transgressions." I recited the first verse of Psalm 51 from memory. Mom had taught it to me when I first became a Christian.

Verse two was the part I *really* needed: "Wash away all my iniquity and cleanse me from my sin."

"Holly? You all right?" Carrie asked, coming into my room. She'd broken our rule about entering without knocking, but it didn't matter.

"I've been a total jerk about Zachary," I said. "But you, Carrie . . . you've been his friend." I reached up and hugged her there on the floor.

"Goody," she said. "I wanna be his best friend. But what's wrong with him?"

B-E-E-P! the smoke detector wailed.

"The pizza!" I yelled as I skipped down the steps two at a time. I grabbed two potholders and pulled the black pizza out of the hot oven.

"Carrie, get Zachary out of this smoke!" I shouted as I rushed the burnt mess out to the trash behind the house. Leaving the baking tray and potholders on top of the trash can, I raced back to the front of the house.

What a relief to see Zachary sitting with Carrie on the porch swing!

He adjusted his baseball cap and grinned at me. "*Now* what's for supper?" he asked.

"I'll think of something. But first you need one of these," I said, pulling the pills out of my pocket.

Carrie ran to get a glass of water.

"Open all the kitchen windows," I called to her, propping the screen door open.

Here I was, alone with Mr. Tate's kid. He was pushing off the redwood porch with his toe, making the swing sway gently. He looked up at me and adjusted his cap.

"Uh, Zachary," I began. "I've treated you pretty lousy lately, and I'm sorry. You probably don't know it, but I think you're really brave." It felt good to apologize. I reached out my hand to him. "Friends?"

He nodded and smiled a toothless grin. His hand was much hotter than I expected.

"You're warm!" I touched his forehead, like Mom always did when I had a fever. My hand felt cool against his face. He *was* feverish.

"My neck hurts," he said.

"Where?" I was surprised to feel the swollen glands where he pointed. Really swollen. "How long has it hurt?" My heart pounded in my ears.

"Since this morning," he said, his face pink.

I helped him inside and told Carrie to bring the thermometer instead of the cold water.

"Coming!" she yelled.

I felt numb. Not too numb to take care of Zach, though. I had lots to make up for.

Carrie brought the thermometer. Slipping it into his mouth, I hoped for the best. Temperatures that zoomed past the tiny arrow—the one marking 98.6 degrees—made me nervous.

Carrie and I waited silently. The minutes crawled by as I kept checking my watch. Finally, I took the thermometer from Zach's mouth and held it steady. The mercury was way past the arrow. It stopped at 102 degrees! Acting calmly, I placed the thermometer on the coffee table.

Zachary looked up at me with his watery, bloodshot eyes. "It's high, isn't it?"

"You have a fever," I said, trying not to upset him. "And it's past time for these." I pulled the pill container out of my pocket.

"Here you go," Carrie said, handing him a glass of water.

We hovered over this frail seven-year-old as if he were our own sick brother. Zach popped his pill like a pro. Then he sipped some water as we watched.

"I'm hungry—let's eat," Carrie said.

I wondered if I should call Mom at the hospital. I checked my watch. They'd been gone less than an hour.

Carrie went to the kitchen and pulled out fixings for sandwiches. But I didn't feel hungry. Zach's disease scared me. Aunt Marla had lost her fight with cancer last winter. I'd used up a whole wad of tissues at her funeral. Now here was Zach with the same thing, and he was only seven years old!

The phone rang. It was Mom!

"Thank goodness it's you," I said quietly.

"What's wrong, honey?"

"It's Zach. He has a fever and his glands are swollen way up."

There was silence.

"Mom?"

"Just a minute, Holly." Her voice sounded muffled, like she was talking to someone in the background. At last, she said, "We'll be right home." She hung up.

This was worse than I thought. I tiptoed over to Zach. Carrie had made him a sandwich, but after a few bites he'd lost interest. Looking up through droopy eyes, he said, "Talk to Jesus for me, Holly."

I knelt beside him and prayed. About his lumps, about his fever, and since I wasn't sure if he knew about the cancer, I said, "Lord, help the pill to work in all the right places."

Zach liked that. He smiled and faded off to sleep.

Dashing to my room, I took my secret prayer list out of hiding and curled up in my window seat. I wrote Zachary's name at the very top. *He* was first. Before Daddy and summer plans. Before Danny Myers and everything else on the list.

"I'm ashamed, Lord," I prayed. "I'm sorry for being so selfish. You know all about this summer and Daddy. If you want me to go, I know you'll work it out, in your way and in your time. It's up to you now. Amen."

Whew! I felt fabulous deep down—knowing that I was trusting God to handle things. Besides, there was plenty to do in Dressel Hills this summer. Like getting Zach well. And having a better attitude towards Mr. Tate.

Hearing the front door open, I raced downstairs to meet Mom and Mr. Tate. They were leaning over Zach, still sound asleep on the living room couch.

Whispering to Mr. Tate, Mom handed him some paper to write on. He stared blankly at it, then reached for the cordless phone.

"Will Zach be okay?" I asked Mom.

"He'll be going back to the hospital," she explained, hugging me close. Then, "Holly, how high was his fever?"

"102 degrees," I said.

"The doctor will want this information," she said, jotting it down on a piece of paper.

Carrie looked worried. "When is he going?"

Mom stared at Zach's father, across the room. "Mike, uh, Mr. Tate will take him tonight as soon as he talks to the doctor on call."

"Tonight?" Carrie asked.

Mom nodded.

"Is he worse?" I asked, eager to tell Mom I knew about the cancer.

Mom led Carrie and me into the kitchen. "Zachary's in trouble," she said. "He has leukemia, and his immune system is very weak. He's picked up another flu bug, too, which is dangerous now."

"Why didn't you tell us this before?" I asked.

"We didn't want to frighten you. You had already lost your Aunt Marla to cancer and . . ." Her voice trailed off. I understood. She was afraid if we knew Zachary was dying, we might treat him differently—be afraid to get to know him. But now I wished I had been told.

I filled Mom's favorite mug with water and slid it into the microwave oven. Right about now she needed some peppermint tea to help her get through. It was obvious how much she cared for Zachary . . . and his father.

Mom motioned for me to sit down at the bar. "I've been so busy with Zachary these past weeks that I've neglected both of you," she said. "Most of my so-called dates with Mike have been spent over at their house comforting Zachary."

"Why you, Mom?" I asked.

"I've become very fond of him," she said, smoothing her hair back. "I want to make a difference in his life if I can."

"Then it's not that you like Mr. Tate as a boyfriend?" I held my breath, hoping I was right.

"I didn't say that," Mom said softly.

Just then we heard Zach heading to the bathroom, moaning.

"Oh, dear," Mom said, rushing after him.

I wanted to put my fingers in my ears to keep out the sounds of his sickness. Poor Zach. Having nausea like that was worse than almost anything. I remembered being sick last winter, and how I'd rather die than vomit. But Zach had to live with it all the time. I shivered, thinking about it.

Mr. Tate was off the phone now. He went upstairs to Zach in the bathroom.

Carrie and I sat like stiff soldiers at the kitchen bar. Her eyes began to fill with tears. "I–is Zachary gonna die?" she asked.

"I don't know," I said softly.

After a while, the three of them came down. Mr. Tate carried Zach out to the car. Mom followed. Carrie and I stood on the porch, too scared to move.

When they left, Mom came up and put her arms around us. "He'll spend the night at the hospital here, then they'll take him to the Denver Children's Hospital in the morning."

Dusk was coming fast. Twilight, Grandma Meredith called it. A faint smell of wood smoke tinged the air. The mountains looked dark against the red sky as twinkly lights showed up in one house, then another.

Looking at the lighted windows, I wondered how many other houses had sad, sick kids living in them. And how many of those kids talked to God about it.

ELEVEN

"Time for pj's," Mom said as we came into the house arm in arm. "Meet me in my room in five minutes."

Carrie and I raced to our rooms. Important stuff was going to be discussed tonight! I threw on my nightshirt, wondering what more Mom was going to tell us. I hoped it wasn't something more about Mr. Tate. I was doing my best to accept him, but I needed more time to get used to him.

I dashed for Mom's room, beating Carrie and claiming a spot on the bed nearest Mom.

Carrie dragged in with her mermaid . . . the present from Mr. Tate. "Can we get Zach a big Sebastian Crab to cheer him up?" she asked.

"Let's find out if he has one first," Mom said.

"He doesn't; I know it," she insisted.

Mom had that faraway look in her eyes that means she's planning things a zillion miles an hour. "Hand me my address book," she said.

I reached for it on her nightstand.

She found the M's and opened it, holding the place with her finger. "I want you girls to listen carefully," she said. "When I'm finished, both of you will have a chance to talk."

Just as I had guessed, this *was* important.

"If things go as planned, Mike, uh, Mr. Tate, will accompany Zachary to Denver. He'll stay there until he's much better and ready to come home."

I could see tears glistening in her eyes. This wasn't easy for her to talk about.

She continued, "I'll call Grandma Meredith tonight to see if she can get a plane out tomorrow. If she can come stay with you girls, then I'll go to Denver for a week to be near Zachary."

Flipping through the address book, she found another number. "Maybe I can stay with my friend from grad school. She and her husband live a few miles from the hospital."

For some strange reason, I remembered Mom's tea in the kitchen. "Just a minute," I said. I got off the bed and headed downstairs.

I took the cup from the microwave. It was still hot. Dipping the tea bag into the water, I stirred in a teaspoon of honey. The way she liked it.

Gingerly, I stepped up the stairs, the mug brimming with peppermint tea. It was the least I could do for Mom.

When I got back, Carrie looked like she'd been crying. I wished she wouldn't. It was hard enough for Mom.

"Any questions?" Mom asked, looking first at Carrie, then at me.

"Do you have to go, Mommy?" Carrie asked.

Mom took a long sip on her tea. "I really don't have to." She sighed. "But I want to be there for Mike while Zachary is getting treatment. And I hope my presence will help Zachary, too. He needs someone . . . a woman's touch."

She was probably thinking about him not having a mother, and wanting to fill that void. What she really meant to say was that he needed a *mother's* touch.

"Holly, how do you feel about it?" She touched my hand.

"I'm glad Zachary will have you near him," I said. "You have what he needs, Mom."

Tears came up again. She wiped them away. "Come here, you angels." She smothered us with hugs.

While Mom called her college friend in Denver, we sat on her bed, listening. Afterwards, Carrie pushed the buttons for Grandma's phone number. She talked for a while, then it was my turn.

"Haven't had a letter from you, Holly, for quite some time," Grandma said.

"Sorry, Grandma. I've been real busy here. But school's out now, and I'll have more time to write."

"When are you coming to see us?" she asked.

"Uh, Grandma? Here's Mom." I handed the phone to her. It was time for Mom to tell Grandma about the plan.

Shortly, we heard Mom say that Grandma would be delighted to come and stay with her beautiful granddaughters. Then Mom was silent for a long time. Grandma must have had something on her mind.

In the middle of the silence, Mom pointed to the door, which meant Carrie and I should give her privacy and leave the room. "Shut the door," she mouthed to us.

In the hallway, we stood, not breathing, trying to hear Mom's side of the conversation.

Nothing.

"What do you think's going on?" Carrie whispered.

"Come in my room and wait," I said. "See this?" I led her to my window seat—the thinking place. "When life gets too hard to figure out, I sit here and talk to God. Sometimes I think first, then I pray. But telling him everything is real important."

"What kind of things?" Carrie asked, squeezing in beside me on the window seat.

"It's different for everyone. Sometimes I pray about my school grades."

"Does it help you get A's?"

"Praying *and* doing my homework does." I reached for a brush and began braiding her hair. "But being close to God is the best part. I don't always ask for things. Sometimes I just like to share everything with him. It's like talking to a good friend, the best friend in the whole world."

"Like you and Andie?" she said.

"Closer than that."

"My best friend is Zachary," she said. "Tonight he told me that people think he's dying, but he's going to fool them."

"More than anything, I hope he does," I said, standing up. "I wonder if Mom's still on the phone." I brushed my own hair, getting it ready for a braid.

"I'll go listen in the crack." Carrie grinned.

She headed down the hallway. I couldn't help but peek around the corner and watch as she squatted near the door and put her ear to the crack. Her head bumped the door, making it squeak open. Mom covered the phone with her hand and said, "Go ahead and get in bed, honey. We'll talk tomorrow. Good night." She blew a kiss.

Carrie came back to tell me what I'd already overheard. "What do you think Grandma's telling Mommy?" she asked.

"Maybe catching up on the family news," I said, curious at the long conversation. "'Night, Carrie."

She scampered off to her room.

I turned the light off and slipped under the sheets, propping Bearie-O up close to me in the darkness.

What *was* going on? I hoped it wasn't something about Grandpa's health. That's *all* we needed.

Suddenly, I was hungry. Skipping supper was not my style. I went to search the kitchen for a snack. Peanut butter crackers would do. And a glass of milk. There were celery and carrot sticks in the fridge. They'd be cold and crunchy. Perfect.

I turned the light off in the kitchen and sat at the bar, my eyes slowly getting used to the darkness. Goofey nuzzled his furry body against my bare legs. I reached down to pet his head. "You need some lovin'?" I asked.

He purred his answer.

"Come here, little one." I picked him up and put him on my lap. He curled into a ball, relishing the late-night attention. "Mommy's busy upstairs. You miss snuggling on her bed?"

Pur-r-r. Sure do, he seemed to say.

Curling up on Mom's bed was a treat. When I was sad or sick, that's where I wanted to be. One night I had slept with Mom all night. Carrie, too. The night Daddy left.

The double bed had been crowded. Carrie had insisted on bringing Goofey in the bed with all of us. I clung to Bearie-O all night, sobbing whenever I woke up. Mom got pushed to the edge when I had a bad dream, and Carrie's knees were in my back. So Mom and I ended up sleeping on the floor in sleeping bags. I remembered snuggling next to her as Goofey purred his kitty song above us in Mom's bed.

I was so hurt and confused. I loved Daddy and never thought anything could go wrong with his love for us.

Four years passed without a word from him. And then, the day before my thirteenth birthday—

at Aunt Marla's funeral—I saw him again. How handsome he had looked in his navy blue pin-striped suit! Saundra, his new wife, accompanied him as we rode together in the limo to the graveside service. Not exactly the perfect place for a girl to meet her long-lost dad.

Saundra had worn bright red lipstick and gloves. Something about her glamorous ways must've made Carrie say she wasn't as sweet as Mom. But it's hard to beat a mother who's an angel. Not because she's perfect or prettier than other mothers—even though she is—but because her beauty is *inside,* too. No wonder Mr. Tate wanted to be around her so much.

And Zachary? How could he resist her love?

Goofey jumped off my lap as Mom's footsteps padded down the stairs. I flicked on the kitchen light. She didn't need to know I was sitting here in the dark, daydreaming about the past.

"Can't you sleep?" she asked, stroking my braid.

"Too hungry." I finished off the peanut butter crackers and milk, hoping to hear about her long phone conversation.

Mom pulled out a bar stool. She lifted her hair off the back of her neck and held it there for a moment. "Holly-Heart, I have something to tell you. I'm sure you'll be very happy."

I leaned forward on my elbows. "What is it?"

She breathed deeply, like she wasn't certain how she should say it. Then it spilled out. "I've decided to let you go to California to visit your father."

"Really? You have?" *Unbelievable!*

"Yes," she said. "But there are some conditions to it."

I was all ears. I leaned forward, almost losing my balance.

"Grandma will arrive here tomorrow afternoon, then if it suits your father—she's calling him now—she'll fly to California with you and Carrie on Monday and stay with you there for about two weeks."

"Oh, thank you, Mom." I hugged her, feeling like a little kid inside. "Thank you for changing your mind."

"I've known how much you wanted to go, Holly. This just seemed to make sense . . . the timing . . . while I'm in Denver with Zachary."

There had to be more to this. "Did Grandma help you decide?" I asked.

Mom's laughter, warm and gentle, touched me. I was right, Grandma had tons to do with her decision. "You know me well, Holly-Heart. I feel much better about you going with Grandma."

"And Carrie?"

"And Carrie," she said, with resolve. "You'll watch out for her, won't you?"

"You know I will, Mom."

The phone rang.

Mom went to the desk in the corner of the kitchen and picked up the cordless phone. "Hello?" Mom said. "Yes?"

I watched her face.

"That sounds good. I know Holly is thrilled about it. Yes . . . she's right here." She turned to me. "It's your father."

"Hi, Daddy," I said, not fully realizing all that had just happened.

"Looks like things are working out for you and Carrie to visit. We're looking forward to it."

"Me, too." I tried to picture myself in the big beach house. "I can't wait."

"I feel the same way," he said. "And it'll be wonderful seeing Grandma again, too. Maybe we should fly Grandpa out and have a family reunion."

"Maybe Andie could come too," I said, joking.

"Who's Andie?"

"Just kidding, Daddy. She's my best friend."

"You'll have to fill me in on all your friends."

I couldn't imagine him being interested in hearing about Andie, or a super-Christian like Danny Myers.

"This is all happening so fast," I said.

"It'll be wonderful having you girls here. Your step-brother is anxious to meet you both."

I'd completely forgotten about him. "How old is he?"

"Tyler's nine," he said. "He's already making plans to entertain you."

I couldn't say I was anxious to meet Saundra's son, especially if he was anything like her. Well, I'd just have to wait and see.

I said good-bye to Daddy, kissed Mom good night, and pranced off to bed. I wouldn't get much sleep tonight, but who cared? I was going to California!

TWELVE

The next morning I woke up early. Life was too exciting to stay in bed. This afternoon I was going to ride up Copper Mountain with Danny, and on Monday I was going to see my dad!

God had answered my prayer so fast, my head was spinning with the speediness of it . . . like getting a fax back from God. I couldn't wait to tell Danny about my latest miracle.

Sitting up in bed, I opened my devotional book. The Scripture was Psalm 18:30, "As for God, his way is perfect." No kidding! If I had tried to put the trip together this fast, well . . . it was obvious who was in charge here.

After breakfast, I called Andie. "Can you come right over?" I asked.

"Too early," she complained. "I'm sleeping in."

I assured her it was extremely important. "Besides," I said, "you have all summer to get caught up on sleep."

After I hung up, I loaded dirty clothes into the washer and cleaned up the kitchen while Mom and Carrie slept.

Boy, was Carrie's summer turning out radically different than she thought! Tagging along with me to California was the perfect answer to all her fears. Surf, sun, and Daddy awaited. Two days away!

At last, Andie arrived, her dark curly hair still wet from her shower.

"What took so long?" I said, opening the door.

"Had to clean my room. Mom's in a spotless mood," she grumbled.

"Want to help me clean mine?" I laughed.

No way, her frown said.

"What did you drag me out of bed for?" she asked.

"I'll tell you. C'mon, let's take a walk." I didn't want Mom to hear Andie fussing about the latest turn of events.

"Where to?" she asked.

"The library."

"Won't be open yet." She looked at her watch. "Too early for anyone sane to be out of bed on the first day of summer vacation."

"Guess Carrie and Mom are saner than both of us," I muttered, as we left the house.

"You guys stay up late?"

"Yeah . . . some scary stuff happened with

Zachary while I was sitting for him last night. He's real sick." I paused, then I said, "Because of that, I'm going to California in two days. My grandma's flying in this afternoon, and then she and Carrie and I are going to see my dad."

Andie stopped dead in her tracks. "Holly, are you crazy? What's that bratty kid got to do with you going to California?" She stood in front of me with her hands on her hips, as if she dared me to take one more step.

"Mom wants to be near him while he stays in the hospital in Denver, so Grandma's taking care of us, and—oh, Andie, I know it sounds complicated, but the way I see it . . . it's a miracle!"

"What are you talking about?"

It wouldn't be easy convincing her that God could use something as bad as Zach's illness and turn it around so I could go to California.

"It's like that verse in Romans," I explained. "All things *do* work together for good, because we love God."

At last, we proceeded down the sidewalk. Andie's fast pace told me she wasn't one bit happy with me. "I love God too, Holly. What happens when *I* pray that you'll stay here this summer? That's for *my* good, like in the verse, right?"

Andie had a point.

"It's only for a couple weeks," I said meekly.

"Two weeks? Holly, that's forever!"

By the look on Andie's face, this was going to be a problem between us, no matter how long or short my visit was.

"I'm going to California, and that's the end of it," I said.

"Whatever," she said angrily.

"Put yourself in my place for once," I said.

"Right," she muttered.

Overhead, a jet left a vapor trail behind, as it climbed up, up over the mountains—reminding me of the trip ahead, and the short time I had to get ready.

I suggested we run back to my house, without stepping on any cracks in the sidewalk. "Don't want to break your mother's back, do you?" I said, trying to chase away the dark mood that hung over Andie. Giggling, I pushed her onto some cracks.

Not so deep inside, we were still kids. Good thing Danny wasn't around to see it, though. I doubt that the giggling and jumping would do much for his impression of me. Unless, of course, there was a logical reason for it.

Logical. That described Danny perfectly. Everything he did was carefully thought out. Even the way he expressed himself and the way he treated his friends. Just knowing I was one of his closest friends made me want to improve my posture—hold my head up, walk tall, throw my shoulders back a little more.

"You're really weird," Andie scoffed at the way I was walking. "What are you doing?"

"Oh, nothing." She didn't *always* have to know what I was thinking.

"Looks to me like you're developing a shape, Holly."

"You're kidding, right?"

"You should walk around like that all the time."

"Thanks, I think." What did my best girlfriend notice that I'd missed? Or was she being sarcastic?

"No kidding, Holly. You're blossoming. That's what my mother calls it. Who knows, in a couple months *it* could happen . . . you could become a woman."

I really and truly hoped so. I was tired of looking like the only praying mantis around. Guess seventh grade girls think more about their bodies than boys do. For sure more than eighth and ninth grade girls. *They've* already got their curves. But I figured if a girl like me could survive the seventh grade where you feel all scrambled up, like in a giant mixing bowl, I could make it through till I blossomed and *it* happened.

"Look out!" Andie yelled. "There's tons of cracks coming up."

We'd turned onto Downhill Court, my street. Part of the sidewalk was bricked, making it almost impossible to run and still miss the cracks. The street was still quiet. Too early for activity. The laziness of summer had come.

"I'd rather starve than eat *that* for breakfast," Andie said to Carrie, who sat on the front porch swing nibbling on a nectarine.

Carrie held up the rosy colored fruit. "There's nothing wrong with this," she said. "Here, try a bite."

"Uh-uh," Andie said, holding her stomach. "You didn't wipe your spit off."

"Don't be gross in front of my little sister," I warned.

"Oh, give me a break, Holly." Andie plopped down on the swing beside Carrie.

"Okay, if you don't *break* the swing," I said, laughing.

Mom came outside, carrying a tray of toast and jelly. And glasses filled with milk. "Anybody hungry?"

"I am," Carrie said, reaching for the tray.

"No thanks, I better go," said Andie, getting up from the swing, making it creak again. "Have to baby-sit my brothers while my mother runs errands. See you at Copper Mountain."

I nodded. "How much money do we need for the gondola ride?" I asked, forgetting what the youth pastor had told us last week.

"Not sure. But I'll call you." Andie sauntered down the redwood steps and waved.

"Better get busy and start packing for California, Holly-Heart," Mom said. "If you don't start planning, you'll come up short on time." She poured more milk for Carrie.

"I'll have everything packed in time," I said.

Carrie wiped her mouth. "Where's she going?"

It was then I realized Mom hadn't told Carrie about our exciting travel plans.

"To California," Mom said calmly. "And so are you."

"I am?" Carrie raised her eyebrows.

I hurried to sit on the swing with her, grabbing her hand. "It's going to be so fabulous, Carrie. We'll walk along the beach, shell hunting. Maybe you'll find some pretty ones to bring home. And . . ."

"Why are we going?" she asked.

Then Mom rehashed the whole amazing story. "So . . . I feel it's a good time for both of you to visit your father. Your grandma will fly out with you while I'm in Denver with Zachary at the Children's Hospital. Everything's set."

Carrie was quiet. I didn't know if she was too shocked to speak, or just still too sleepy.

"Daddy has a stepson a little older than you, named Tyler. We'll both get to meet him for the first time," I said, hoping for a response.

Carrie stood up and placed her empty glass on the tray. "I'm not going," she said. "I want to stay home. What if Zach gets worse? I can't leave him now. I won't." She reached for the screen door.

"Carrie, you *have* to go," I wailed.

"I'll handle this," Mom said, getting up and going inside after her.

Oh great, I thought. *Now she's acting ridiculous.* There was absolutely nothing Carrie could do to help Zach by staying home.

I sat there in the morning stillness, listening to the gentle humming sounds of insects as they sent secret messages back and forth to each other. Leaning my head back, I could see the clouds playing Follow-the-Leader

Slam! It was the screen door.

Mom stood there with her arms crossed. "Carrie simply does not want to go. She's upstairs crying about it, and I don't see the sense in forcing her."

I stuck my feet up under me on the porch swing. "That's weird. Yesterday she didn't want to be left behind with a bunch of sitters."

"There won't be any sitters around, with you and Grandma here . . . until I get back from Denver."

"Grandma? Me?" *What was happening*?

"Holly, things have changed," she said, abruptly. "The trip is off. I'm sorry."

"Why?" I cried. "Just because Carrie doesn't want to go? What about *me*?"

Mom pulled a dead leaf off the geranium plant.

"What about Daddy?" I continued. "He's expecting us."

"Your father will have to adjust his plans."

"Why can't I go by myself? Why does everything have to change because of Carrie?"

"Holly, listen," Mom said. "Carrie's crying because she's afraid."

"But there's nothing to be afraid of," I said. "She's acting like a big baby, and I can't believe you're letting her."

Mom eased down into the porch chair. "There *are* things to be afraid of, and Carrie's not the only one who has fears. I struggle with them too."

"Like what?" I didn't really care what, I just wanted to talk sense into Mom. And fast.

"Like losing you, Holly-Heart."

"How could that possibly happen?" I shot back. She was talking in riddles now.

She sighed, staring down into her lap. "Maybe you'd end up wanting to live with your father."

I wanted to laugh. "That's the silliest thing I've heard all day! Why would I want to do that?"

Mom blew her nose. She was crying about all this! But I still said, "If you want to know the truth, Mom, when it comes right down to it, there's only one thing that could make me want to leave Dressel Hills. And that's if you and Mr. Tate decide to get married!" There, I'd said it—my greatest fear.

"What a terrible thing to say, Holly," Mom said, jumping off her chair. "You have no right to threaten me with such a thing. Now go to your room."

"I'd rather go to California," I shouted.

"It's no use," Mom said, turning to go. "It's out of the question now."

The porch swing swayed as I gritted my teeth. So much for miracles and divine fax machines.

THIRTEEN

I was crushed. How could things be so perfect one minute, and so crazy the next? Lying on the porch swing, I stared up at the sky. Puffs of cotton dotted the blue. They seemed close enough to touch. Squinting one eye shut, I reached up, aiming for the smallest cloud in the bunch. My squinting squeezed out a tear. Then another. In seconds, the cloud I reached for was a blurry blob. I dropped my arm and covered my face with it, letting out the sobs.

How could Mom do this to me?

And Daddy . . . When would I ever see him again? If not this summer, when? Once school started there would be no time. Eighth grade was much harder than seventh. Everyone said so.

The phone rang. I listened through the window,

hoping it was Daddy or someone else talking sense to Mom besides me.

The screen door opened. "It's Andie, for you," Mom said, handing the portable phone to me.

"Hello," I said, wiping the tears off my face.

"You sound morbid," she said.

"Promise not to cheer if I tell you?"

"Maybe, maybe not," she said with a giggle.

"It's not funny, Andie. The trip's off."

"You're not going?" She was obviously happy.

"No." I explained my dilemma.

"Well, I called to find out what you're wearing to the skyride," she said, ignoring my woes. "Don't forget, Danny'll be there."

Butterfly flutters still tickled inside when I heard his name. "That's nice," I said calmly.

"I know you better than that," she said. "You really can't wait to see him, can you?"

She was right. "What about you, Andie? Got your eyes on Billy Hill?"

"He's cool. I hope Danny invites him."

Mom was giving me a signal.

"Got to go now," I said.

"Remember, wear pink," Andie said.

Mom stood by the kitchen door. She pulled her keys out of her purse. "I have to pick up some groceries for tonight." She looked at me searchingly. "I'll be back shortly."

I turned away. I didn't want to talk to her. She'd spoiled my summer dreams with her crazy fears. Now all I could look forward to was the gondola ride with Danny—if the Miller twins didn't get to him first.

♥ ♥ ♥

I'd seen crowded parking lots before, but this one was hopping. It seemed like every teen in the youth group—and their friends—had shown up to ride the gondolas up Copper Mountain.

I scanned the cars for Danny. Was he here?

Billy Hill was heading up the walkway leading to the ticket booth. I grabbed Andie's arm. "Look who's here," I whispered, popping a chunk of bubble gum into my mouth.

"Wanna ride with me, girls?" It was Jared, sneaking up behind us. As usual.

"Guess again," Andie retorted.

"Spunky. I like that," he said.

Andie fluffed her curls. "Don't you have a date or something?

"Sure." He grabbed my arm playfully. "How 'bout you, Holly? You look lonely."

"Look again." I blew a bubble in his face.

"Thanks, think I will." Jared stepped back, playfully turning his head this way and that. Admiring me.

"Oh, ple-ase," Andie groaned.

Then I spotted Danny's auburn hair as he climbed out of the church van. I wondered if he was going to ride the gondola with our youth pastor. *Please come over and talk to me,* I thought, excitement bubbling inside.

Andie and I purchased our tickets and stood

looking up at the apparatus that held the gondolas on the cable line. It looked wobbly to me. The best thing about them was they were enclosed, with windows all around. Very private. Even though there was room for four, I hoped Danny and I would ride alone—just the two of us.

"Hi, Holly," Danny said, arriving in time for boarding.

"Hi," I said.

"Step right this way," the guy working the gondolas called. He pointed where I should wait for the next car to come around. "Who's riding with this young lady?"

Danny stepped up beside me. "I am," he said, grinning.

I caught my breath. What a smile he had. And the twinkle in his green eyes did strange things to my heartbeat.

The worker steadied the gondola as it came around, and I stepped in. Danny climbed in and sat in the seat across from me.

"Keep the window halfway down," the worker told us. "No roughhousing, leaning out the window, or throwing objects from the gondola. Okay—you're off!" He slid the door shut and locked it behind us.

My hand clutched my purse. I wished for something to grab onto. No roughhousing—no problem! I wasn't exactly crazy about heights, and I was hoping our weight would evenly balance the car on the cables so it wouldn't swing.

The car swung away from the wooden platform

and out into the open air. I looked down at the parking lot, milling with people. But as we climbed higher, their faces faded, becoming tiny dots. We passed over the tops of trees, blue-green pine and quaking aspen. The sun was shining, and a breeze crept through the window, smelling of damp earth and pine needles.

The gondola rumbled past the first set of terminals, shaking us. I shivered a little and looked over at Danny.

"First time on the skyride?" he asked.

I nodded. "I rode on one when I was little. Mom says Daddy took me for a ride on the Fourth of July, but I don't remember."

"You miss him, don't you?" His voice was gentle.

"More than ever."

"You seem a little sad today," he said.

I didn't want to spoil the gondola ride, but I *was* feeling lousy. And Danny had listened so well when I told him about my plans for California. So I told him everything that had happened in the last twenty-four hours—about Zachary and his cancer, our plans to go to California with Grandma, and how Carrie chickened out. "It seemed like God was working everything out," I said, "and then Carrie had to mess it all up."

"Maybe God has a better plan for your trip," Danny said. "Is your mom going to let you go later in the summer?"

I made a face. "I doubt it. Mom's being totally unreasonable about it."

"Maybe she's worried. Mothers do that a lot, you know."

"No kidding," I said, recalling Mom's number-one reason for calling the whole thing off. Ridiculous!

The gondola began to sway. Not daring to peek down for a minute, I stared out my window at treetop level. Towering pines pointed to the blue sky, and Copper Mountain rose before us in all its splendor. Inside this tiny compartment, I felt nervous about being up as high as the birds, dangling precariously above jagged rocks and forested canyons.

"Nervous?" Danny asked.

I nodded.

"It won't be much longer," he said, gazing out the window behind me.

Slowly, I turned to look. Approaching us, steadily, was a steep cliff. As we came closer, the cables veered up, up. Up! Swallowing my bubble gum, I looked away from the terrain beneath us and back at Danny.

"We have to come back *down* that cliff, don't we?" I said.

He nodded. "But we could sing our favorite songs from choir tour to keep you from thinking about it."

I realized Danny wanted to ride back down the mountain with me!

"If we sing in two-part harmony, it might be easy to forget the distance between us and the ground. We'll concentrate on the distance in our pitches," he laughed.

At last, the gondola reached the top of Copper Mountain and swung onto another wooden platform. We climbed out carefully and took the steps from the platform down to the ground. Since we were among the first to arrive, we had some time to spend before the whole group gathered. A short devotional was scheduled first, then a hike, followed by the sky ride down.

A walkway made of woodchips led to five hiking trails, and a sign pointed the way to a nearby lookout site. "Let's wait over there for the others," Danny said, walking toward the lookout.

The lookout was on top of a large flat rock, ringed with an iron fence. We stood at the fence and looked down. Far below, Dressel Hills snuggled in its peaceful boring valley. Surrounded by shining mountains, the village seemed to taunt me. *You're stuck here for the summer,* it teased. *This is as far away as you'll ever get from me.*

Soon the sound of laughter announced the arrival of the others. In a few minutes we were gathered around Pastor Rob as he shared a quick devotional.

Afterwards, Andie and I headed for the outhouses near the crest of the hill.

"Are you and Billy getting along?" I asked.

She tried to act sophisticated—not an easy task for Andie. "We rode up together. That's something, I guess."

I pinched my nose shut as we came within a few

feet of the girls' outhouse. "Whew," I said. "It stinks!"

Andie said she'd guard the door while I went inside. It was an old wooden outhouse, with a toilet lid built into a box. Flies buzzed around deep down inside the opening. Smelling the stench was enough to make me change my mind about using this facility.

"It's too nasty in here," I shouted. "I'm coming out!" I pushed on the wooden door.

It stuck! I pounded on the door. "Get me out of here, Andie!"

"What's wrong?" she called.

"The door's stuck—I can't get it open!" I tried again. No luck.

The door jiggled a little. "I'm trying," Andie said from outside.

More door jiggling and . . . groaning.

"Guess you're in there for the summer," Andie said. "I never would've picked *this* option, but it'll sure work to keep you in Dressel Hills."

"Stop it, Andie Martinez," I hollered. "You know I'm not going anywhere this summer! Besides, the smell in here is sickening."

"I'm doing my best," she called.

"Get some help if you can't do it yourself!"

"How about Danny and Billy? Looks like they're waiting near the trailhead."

"Just get them up here," I said, dying for a whiff of fresh mountain air.

"Wait here."

"Right, like I can leave or something!"

Stranded on the top of Copper Mountain, stuck in a stinky old outhouse was not my idea of fun. This had to go down in my journal as one of the most embarrassing moments of all time!

Fearful thoughts nagged at me. What if they couldn't get me out before dark? What if I had to spend the night up here . . . alone?

Footsteps and voices!

I peered through the splintery cracks in this wretched excuse for a restroom. Couldn't see a thing.

Don't freak out, I told myself, trying not to think about the insects and snakes and who knows what else lived in this miserable place.

Danny called, "Still in there, Holly?"

"Where else would I be?"

"There's only one *other* way out of there," Andie said.

Laughter! Was the whole youth group outside watching?

"Now get ready to pull . . . hard," I heard Danny say.

"Don't knock the old thing over," Andie said. "We want Holly out of there alive."

I heard a scary sound over in the corner. It was too dark to see. I covered my mouth. Should I scream? Andie would if she were stuck in here. I was sure of it.

Something tickled my head. It was probably a black widow spider!

I froze.

FOURTEEN

Just then the door flung open wide. I squinted into the brightness. "Who's next?" I asked. I stepped down like it was no big deal, even though I really wanted to reach up and kiss the sun.

"Not me, huh-uh," Andie said, backing away. "I'll wait."

"Me, too," said another girl. "Let's get outta here."

The line of waiting girls vanished.

When no one was looking, I grabbed Andie. "Look in my hair."

"What for?" she said.

"Is there a spider or something in it?"

She looked. "There's this." She held up a splinter of wood.

"I want it," I said, pushing it into my jeans pocket. "The perfect souvenir."

Pastor Rob called everyone to join him. "I'll blaze the trail," he announced. We started down a narrow, twisting path.

Danny fell in step behind me. "That was some outhouse experience."

"Nothing like that has ever happened to me," I said. I could laugh about it now—now that I could breathe the smell of pines and see the smile on Danny's face.

The hike was a quick one because so many of us girls needed the restrooms, and none of us were brave enough to set foot in the only other choice . . . the boy's outhouse.

Before I knew it, Danny and I were back on the gondola—alone—for the ride down. Bumpity-lumpity-thump! I held my breath as we drifted down the mountain. The gondola did its thing with the terminal overhead. I couldn't wait to get out of this sky ride.

It was close to suppertime as we skimmed over the tops of the trees. Grandma Meredith would be waiting at home, anxious to greet me. Did she know that Mom worried about me wanting to live with Daddy?

"You're too quiet," Danny said, his eyes searching mine.

"Just thinking."

"Feel like singing?"

I didn't really, but Danny looked so eager, I agreed to.

"Remember our theme song for choir tour?"

"Sure," I said. "Everybody Sing Praises to the

Lord" was a favorite of mine—Danny's too. I sang along as he harmonized with his clear tenor voice, almost forgetting how high we were off the ground. Almost forgetting about California until Danny mentioned it.

"I hope you won't take this wrong, Holly," Danny said.

"What?" I asked.

"I've been thinking a lot about your California trip."

"You have?"

"And I agree with your mother, Holly. You shouldn't go." His eyes had turned serious.

Anger rose in me, and I lashed out at him. "What do you mean, I shouldn't go? How could you say that?"

"You just ought to obey your mother and stay home."

"You have no right to tell me what to do!"

"Don't get mad, Holly," he said. "That's just how I feel."

"Well, you're one hundred percent wrong, and so is my mom!"

He looked surprised at my response. I didn't care. Danny had no right to tell me what to do.

After the sky ride, I hurried over to Mrs. Martinez's car without saying good-bye to Danny. Andie was waiting inside. When we had pulled out of the parking lot and Andie's mom wasn't listening, I poked Andie.

"I have to talk to you," I said. "It's about Danny.

He's being a jerk. He said he doesn't want me going to California."

Andie smiled. "What's wrong with that?"

"He has no right to tell me what to do. We're not really going out together or anything, you know."

"And if you *were* going out, you'd be mad at him for being too possessive. Right? So it doesn't really matter, does it, Holly?" she said. "You want everyone to see things your way or not at all."

"Yeah, right," I said, folding my arms stubbornly. We didn't talk for the rest of the short ride.

Arriving at home, I trudged up the steps and into the house. Grandma Meredith waited with open arms. "Hello, my dear," she said, holding me close.

The tears spilled down my cheeks.

"Why, honey! What's wrong?" She hugged me again. "Come, Holly-Heart, it's time for us to catch up on things." She led me to the family room, and after we were seated on the couch, I let my frustrations pour out.

"What do you think about praying for something you want real bad, Grandma, and it looks like your answer is yes? But then God doesn't let it happen. I was all set to go to California, nearly dying to go, and then Mom changed her mind."

Grandma's face was solemn. "Remember, dear, it's not easy for grown-ups to set their youngsters free, especially to parts unknown," she said.

"Can't you get Mom to change her mind, Grandma?"

"Your mother is making the best decision she can based on the circumstances."

"Yeah, right," I whispered.

"We all long for that first taste of freedom, Holly-Heart," she said. "But now you must think of your mother. She's thinking of *you*."

"Not really. She's letting Carrie's decision change everything. It's not fair."

"Well, it's not really your sister's fault, is it?"

I leaned against Grandma. "It's just that God was working everything out for me. Now where is he?"

"God can't always be blamed for things not turning out the way we want them to."

I sighed. Deep down I knew she was right. God had helped us through tough times, and Mom relied on him when she made decisions. I could count on her no matter what—she was a safe harbor in the hurricanes of my life. No way could I disappoint her now.

"Guess I was wrong about Mom," I said.

Grandma kissed me. Then I hurried upstairs, where I smelled her famous beef and barley stew simmering.

Carrie was still trying to organize her room when I knocked on her door. "Who is it?" she asked.

"Your fairy godmother, who else?"

"I don't want any wishes today," she said.

I laughed at her wit, waiting in the hall for an invitation to enter. "Well?"

"Well what?"

"May I please come in?" I asked.
"What's the magic word?"
"Aw, come on, Carrie, this is stupid."
"The *magic* word," she insisted.
"How should I know? It changes every week." I was getting more irritated by the second.
"Exactly," she answered.
Hmm, now what could be on her mind?
"What about Zachary? Is that the magic word?"
"Nope."
"Summer vacation?"
"That's *two* words."
Exasperating little sister I have. "Ice cream?"
"You're not even close," her voice chimed through the door.
"I give up then," I shouted.
"Holly! Don't be mad," she said, opening the door. "*California*. The magic word's California, and you're going there all by yourself."
I sat on Carrie's bed. "That's not funny, Carrie. Don't you know how badly I wanted to go and you're . . ."
"I'm telling the truth. I really am. Mommy's on the phone with Daddy right now," she said, her eyes growing wide.
I didn't know whether to laugh or cry or dance for joy. So, I did two out of three. "Give me your hands," I shouted, reaching for Carrie and swinging her around.
"What's going on in there?" Mom called from her room.

"Celebration." Oops, I let Carrie's secret slip out.

"I couldn't help it, Mommy," Carrie said when Mom peeked around the corner.

Mom stepped back into the hallway, her eyes squinting. "You're happy, right?" she said to me.

I hugged her hard. "Oh, thank you, thank you. I love you, Mom," I cried.

After hugs and kisses were passed around, Mom sat down. "Before you go off in another direction, Holly-Heart, let's talk. I'll be leaving for Denver tonight. Here's my phone number in case you need to call me." She gave an index card to me. "Zachary has already begun treatment for septicemia."

"Sounds scary. What is it?" I asked.

"His immune system is so weak his body has trouble throwing off germs that cause minor things in healthy people, like colds and sore throats. It's a very serious thing for him to get a bug like this on top of trying to fight cancer."

"Does Zach know?"

"His father has told him enough to satisfy him without scaring him."

I twisted my hair. "Carrie says he's going to fool everyone and live."

"I hope he continues to keep a positive attitude. That's important."

"Mom?" I slid over beside her. "Do *you* think he'll make it?"

"I'm praying he will."

"Me, too," I said, wishing I'd known about Zach months ago. I'd misjudged him completely.

"I have some last-minute packing to do," Mom said, heading back to her room.

I tucked my pink shirt into my jeans. Turning sideways, I stared at Carrie's mirror. Andie was right, I was beginning to blossom. Had anyone else noticed?

I sneaked over to Mom's room. Coming up behind her, I gave her a bear hug. "I'm sorry," I said. "I was wrong about you, Mom. And very selfish."

"I love you, Holly-Heart," she said, turning around. "I'm sorry, too. It's been a difficult time for all of us."

"I resented Mr. Tate for taking you away from us," I said, putting my arm around her. "Then when you said it was Zach taking up so much of your time, I understood better."

"I'm glad you do," she said, stroking my hair.

Grandma and Carrie stood in the doorway. Grandma's eyes glistened as she pulled Carrie close.

Mom closed her suitcase. "Well, dear ones, this is good-bye for a couple weeks. I hope you have a good time with Grandma, Carrie. And Holly, I hope you get to know your father better. Be sweet," Mom said.

"I'll be okay, you'll see," I said. "Thanks for letting me go, Mom. You won't be sorry."

We followed her downstairs to the garage and watched as she backed down the driveway.

I whispered, "I love you, Mom" as she drove away.

It felt good knowing Mom trusted me with this visit. If *she* thought I was grown-up enough, surely Danny would realize how mature I was getting. If he'd just stop trying to run my life!

At church the next day, I told Andie and Danny my good news. "I'm leaving for California tomorrow."

Andie tossed her head. "Go ahead, just leave me all alone. See if I care."

"I'll be back in a month, Andie. It's *not* the end of the world."

She pouted. "Maybe not for you."

Danny's eyes had lost their twinkle. He didn't say anything—just stood there, with his arms folded. Grandma called me away, and I turned to go, leaving Andie and Danny standing in the church foyer.

I spent Sunday afternoon packing. Sunday evening Daddy called one last time to make sure everything was set. "We're excited about your visit, Holly," he said. "Tyler is helping Saundra get your room ready right now."

For the third night in a row, I had trouble sleeping. *No problem,* I thought. *I'll just sleep on Daddy's beach all week long!*

Monday morning, I got up bright and early to shower and fix my hair. Just as I sprayed my bangs one last time, the phone rang.

It was Andie. I knew she'd apologize . . . sooner or later.

"I hope you come back with a good tan," she said.

"Thanks, Andie. You're a true friend."

"Hey, guess what? You'll be back in plenty of time to go rafting with us," she said.

"Really?"

"Yep, Dad changed his vacation just so you could come along," she said.

"That's perfect," I said. "Tell him thanks!"

"I'll really miss you, Holly."

"I'll write," I said. "I promise."

"Call me collect if you meet a cute guy, okay?"

"Maybe, maybe not." I laughed. "See you soon."

After breakfast, Grandma and Carrie helped me haul my stuff out to the car. I squirmed excitedly all the way to the airport. "Turn here," I told Grandma, pointing to the sign for short-term parking.

"I'll drop you off here, Holly," she said pulling up in front of our mini-airport. "Put your luggage on a cart, then get in line while I park the car."

I loaded my bags onto a nearby cart and wheeled it inside. For a small airport, the terminal was buzzing with people. I wondered where everyone was headed on Memorial Day. California was *my* destination! I wanted to boogie all the way to the ticket counter.

"Holly!" Out of the crowd came a familiar voice.

I looked over my pile of luggage to see Danny waving at me.

"Hi," I said, surprised to see him. "What are you doing here?"

"I came to say good-bye," he said. "And to give you this."

He handed me a square envelope.

"What is it?"

"Wait to open it on the plane," he said shyly.

I blushed. "Okay."

My heart did two-and-a-half flipflops as I slipped the envelope into my overnight case.

Danny helped wheel my luggage to the ticket counter. Quickly I filled out address labels for all my bags. Then we stood in awkward silence as the line inched forward.

"Traveling together?" the attendant asked when we arrived at the ticket counter.

Danny began to search for his "ticket," pulling the pocket linings out of his jeans. "Guess you'll have to go on without me, Miss Meredith," he said playfully.

I hammed it up. "Bummer. What a summer!" I handed my ticket to the agent, who seemed concerned about Danny's lost ticket.

"Never mind, sir," Danny said. "I'll catch up with her later."

Danny helped me check the luggage. All but one piece . . . the overnight case. "I'll carry this on, thanks."

He looked at my ticket. "Wow, you'll be in Denver before I ride my bike home," he said.

"Your bike? You rode all the way out here on your bike?"

He nodded. "It was nothing, really."

"Thanks for coming," I said.

"Good-bye, Holly." He turned to go before I could say more.

Grandma and Carrie arrived just as he disappeared through the automatic doors. "I'm all set," I said. "Let's go to gate 4!"

We headed down the short concourse.

"Do you have something to keep you busy while you're on the plane?" Grandma asked.

I tapped the top of my overnight case.

Carrie asked, "What's in there?"

"Something," I said, secretively.

"Let me see!" Carrie said, reaching for it.

"Not in your wildest dreams," I said, dangling the key in front of her nose.

"Holly!" she squealed. "Please?"

"Nope."

"I'll find your journal and read it while you're gone!"

"Do I look dumb enough to leave my secrets behind in my bottom drawer?"

"Aw, phooey," she whined.

"Look, there's Holly's plane," Grandma said, pointing to the small aircraft up ahead. "If you need help when you change planes in Denver, ask a ticket agent."

"I will, Grandma. Don't worry," I said, giving her a quick kiss. "Thanks for bringing me."

"Hurry home," Carrie said, kissing my cheek.

"Bye!" I said, waving to them as I stepped into the portable hallway leading to the plane. I was fabulously excited! And I couldn't wait to see what Danny had given me.

The second I was settled in my seat, I reached for my overnight case. There was Danny's envelope. Carefully, I opened it.

It was a picture of me with a horrible look on my face—the worst picture I'd ever seen of myself!

Then I remembered. Looking closely, I saw the giant green June bug sitting in my hair. How long ago that seemed . . . zillions of summer plans and dreams ago. And some of the best ones were coming true! Here I was—on my way to see Daddy, and Danny had come to see me off at the airport.

A note was attached to the picture.

Dear Holly:

Jared wanted five bucks for this. It was worth it, don't you think? Now no one can blackmail you, can they?

I smiled and continued reading.

Was I ever a jerk last Saturday at Copper Mountain! Yesterday too. Guess I said some pretty selfish things about you staying home this summer. I didn't mean them. What I really meant to say was I'll miss you if you leave.

As always,
Danny

I clasped the note to my heart as the plane sped down the runway for lift-off.

♥ About the Author ♥

Beverly Lewis wrote zillions of secret lists and diary entries (still does!) while growing up in Lancaster County, Pennsylvania. Now she keeps a secret scrapbook for each of her three children to be presented on their 21st birthdays. She and her husband, Dave, and their cock-a-poo, Cuddles, live with their family in Colorado.

A former schoolteacher, Beverly has published over forty short stories and articles in magazines such as *Highlights for Children, Brio, Faith 'n Stuff, Dolphin Log,* and *Guide.* Her hilarious chapter books are titled *Mountain Bikes and Garbanzo Beans* and *The Six-Hour Mystery.*

Plot ideas spring from Beverly's threesome (twins + one = fun!) as well as from her voice and piano students, who eat ice cream and other junk food at monthly performance classes.

Don't Miss the Other Holly's

Holly's First Love

Book #1 0-310-38051-0

The new boy at school threatens to destroy Holly's relationship with her best friend, Andie. Holly has a secret plan, but when it backfires, she learns the meaning of friendship and the miracle of forgiveness.

Secret Summer Dreams

Book #2 0-310-38061-8

Holly wants to visit her father in California for the summer, but the idea doesn't make either her best friend, Andie, or her mother very happy. Holly gets some advice from Danny, who seems to have more than just a big brotherly concern. Will Holly make it to California?

Sealed with a Kiss

Book #3 0-310-38071-5

When Holly and Andie have a pen-pal contest, Holly gets a male pen pal who is in college. To impress him, she lies about her age. He then writes that he is coming to Dressel Hills for a visit. What should Holly do?

The Trouble with Weddings

Book #4 0-310-38081-2

Holly's mother is getting married, and Holly is determined to make it a memorable wedding—against her mother's wishes. Meanwhile, Holly tests her former "first love" to see if he's really changed.

Heart Books in the Series!

CALIFORNIA CHRISTMAS

Book #5 0-310-43321-5

Holly and her sister receive a surprise Christmas invitation to visit their father in California. While there, Holly meets a California surfer, Sean, and her faithfulness to her boyfriend back home is tested.

SECOND-BEST FRIEND

Book #6 0-310-43331-2

When Holly's best friend, Andie, invites her Austrian pen pal to Dressel Hills, jealousy erupts as Christiana moves in on Holly's friendship with Andie.

GOOD-BYE, DRESSEL HILLS

Book #7 0-310-44410-1

Holly is moving away from Dressel Hills, and she has just two weeks to say good-bye to all her friends. She wonders whether to continue a "long-distance" relationship with Jared, or to break it off now. To top it off, the surfer she met in California wants to come visit. What should Holly do?

STRAIGHT-A TEACHER

Book #8 0-310-46111-1

Holly develops a crush on the new teacher at school, and he soon becomes the focus of her attention. Her best friend, Andie, wonders if Holly's lead in the spring musical is a result of the handsome teacher playing favorites. Don't miss this exciting climax of the Holly's Heart series.